"Maresa."

Her name on his lips was a warning. A chance to change her mind.

She understood that she was pushing a boundary. Recognized that he'd just drawn a line in the sand.

"I didn't mind giving up my dream job in Paris to care for Rafe and help my mother recover," she confided, giving him absolutely no context for her comment and hoping he understood what she was saying. "And I will gladly give eighteen years to raise my niece as my own daughter." She'd known it without question the moment Jaden had handed her Isla. "But I'm not sure I can sacrifice the chance to have this kiss."

She'd crossed the boundary. Straight into "certifiable" territory. She must have cried out all her good sense.

His blue eyes simmered with more heat than a St. Thomas summer. He cupped her chin, cradling her face like she was something precious.

"If I thought you wouldn't regret it tomorrow, I'd give you all the kisses you could handle."

* * *

His Accidental Heir
is part of Mills & Boon Desire's Nº1 bestselling series, Billionaires and Babies: Powerful men… wrapped around their babies' little fingers.

HIS
ACCIDENTAL HEIR

BY
JOANNE ROCK

First Published in Great Britain 2017
By Mills & Boon, an imprint of HarperCollins*Publishers*
1 London Bridge Street, London, SE1 9GF

© 2017 Joanne Rock

ISBN: 978-0-263-06921-1

Our policy is to use papers that are natural, renewable and recyclable
products and made from wood grown in sustainable forests. The logging
and manufacturing processes conform to the legal environmental
regulations of the country of origin.

Printed and bound in Great Britain
by CPI Antony Rowe, Chippenham, Wiltshire

Four-time RITA® Award nominee **Joanne Rock** has penned over seventy stories for Mills & Boon. An optimist by nature and a perpetual seeker of silver linings, Joanne finds romance fits her life outlook perfectly—love is worth fighting for. A former Golden Heart® Award recipient, she has won numerous awards for her stories. Learn more about Joanne's imaginative Muse by visiting her website, joannerock.com, or following @joannerock6 on Twitter.

For Barbara Jean Thomas, an early mentor and role model of hard work. Thank you, Barbara, for teaching me the value of keeping my chin up and having faith in myself. During my teens, you were so much more than a boss… You were a friend, a cheerleader and a sometimes mom on those weekend trips with the crew. I'll never forget my visit to New York to see Oprah, courtesy of you! Much love to you, always.

One

"Rafe, I need you in the Antilles Suite today." Maresa Delphine handed her younger brother a gallon jug of bubble bath. "I have a guest checking in who needs a hot bath on arrival, but he isn't sure what time he'll get here."

Her twenty-one-year-old sibling—who'd recently suffered a traumatic brain injury in a car accident—didn't reach to take the jug. Instead, his hazel eyes tracked the movements of a friendly barmaid currently serving a guest a Blackbeard's Revenge specialty drink on the patio just outside the lobby. The Carib Grand Hotel's floor-to-ceiling windows allowed for views of the tiki bar on Barefoot Beach and the glittering Caribbean Sea beyond. Inside the hotel, the afternoon activity had picked up since Maresa's mad dash to the island's sundries shop for the bath products. All of her runners had been busy fulfilling other duties for guests, so she'd made the trip herself. She had no idea what her newest runner—her recovering brother who still needed to work in a monitored environment—had been doing at that hour. He hadn't answered his radio and he needed to get with the program if he wanted to remain employed. Not to mention, Maria might be blamed for his slipups. She was supporting her family, and couldn't afford to lose her job as concierge for this exclusive hotel on a private island off Saint Thomas.

And she really, really needed him to remain employed where she could watch over him. Where he was eligible for better insurance benefits that could give him the long-term follow-up care he would need for years. She knew she held Rafe to a higher standard so that no one on staff could view his employment as a conflict of interest. Sure, the hotel director had approved his application, but she had promised to carefully supervise her brother during his three-month trial period.

"Rafe." She gently nudged her sibling with the heavy container of rose-scented bubbles, remembering his counselor's advice about helping him stay on task when he got distracted. "I have some croissants from the bakery to share with you on your next break. But for now, I really need help. Can you please take this to the Antilles Suite? I'd like you to turn on the hot water and add this for a bubble bath as soon as I text you."

Their demanding guest could stride through the lobby doors any moment. Mr. Holmes had phoned this morning, unsure of his arrival time, but insistent on having a hot bath waiting for him. That was just the first item on a long list of requests.

She checked her slim watch, a gift from her last employer, the Parisian hotel where she'd had the job of her dreams. As much as Maresa loved her former position, she couldn't keep it after her mother's car accident that had caused Rafe's head injury almost a year ago. Going forward, her place was here in Charlotte Amalie to help with her brother.

She refused to let him fail at the Carib Grand Hotel. Her mother's poor health meant she couldn't supervise him at home, for one thing. So having him work close to Maresa all day was ideal.

"I'll go to the Antilles Suite." Rafe tucked the bubble bath under one arm and continued to study the barmaid, a sweet girl named Nancy who'd been really kind to him when Maresa introduced them. "You will call me on the phone when I need to turn on the water."

Maresa touched Rafe's cheek to capture his full attention, her fingers grazing the jagged scar that wrapped beneath his left ear. Her mother had suffered an MS flare-up behind the wheel one night last year, sending her car into a telephone pole during a moment of temporary paralysis. Rafe had gone through the windshield since his seatbelt was unbuckled; he'd been trying to retrieve his phone that had slid into the backseat. Afterward, Maresa had been deeply involved in his recovery and care since their mother had been battling her own health issues. Their father had always been useless, a deadbeat American businessman who worked in the cruise industry and used to visit often, wooing Maresa's mother with promises about coming to live with him in Wisconsin when he saved up enough money to bring them. That had never happened, and he'd checked out on them by the time Maresa was ten, moving to Europe for his job. Yet then, as now, Maresa didn't mind adapting her life to help Rafe. Her brother's injuries could have been fatal that day. Instead, he was a happy part of her world. Yes, he would forever cope with bouts of confusion, memory loss and irritability along with the learning disabilities the accident had brought with it. Throughout it all, though, Rafe was always... Rafe. The brother she adored. He'd been her biggest supporter after her former fiancé broke things off with her a week before their wedding two years ago, encouraging her to go to Paris and "be my superstar."

He was there for her then, after that humiliating experience. She would be there for him now.

"Rafe? Go to the Antilles Suite and I'll text you when it's time to turn on the hot water." She repeated the instructions for him now, knowing it would be kinder to transfer him to the maintenance team or landscaping staff where he could do the same kinds of things every day. But who would watch out for him there? "Be sure to add the bubbles. Okay?"

Drawing in a breath, she took comfort from the soothing scent of white tuberoses and orchids in the arrangement on her granite podium.

"A bubble bath." Rafe grinned, his eyes clearing. "Can do." He ambled off toward the elevator, whistling.

Her relief lasted only a moment because just then a limousine pulled up in front of the hotel. She had a clear view out the windows overlooking the horseshoe driveway flanked by fountains and thick banks of birds-of-paradise. The doormen moved as a coordinated team toward the vehicle, prepared to open doors and handle baggage.

She straightened the orchid pinned on her pale blue linen jacket. If this was Mr. Holmes, she needed to stall him to give Rafe time to run that bath. The guest had been curt to the point of rudeness on the phone, requiring a suite with real grass—and it had to be ryegrass only—for his Maltese to relieve himself. The guest had also ordered a dog walker with three years' worth of references and a groomer on-site, fresh lilacs in the room daily and specialty pies flown in from a shop in rural upstate New York for his bedtime snack each evening.

And that was just for starters. She couldn't wait to see what he needed once he settled in for his two-week stay. These were the kinds of guests that could make or break a career. The vocal kind with many precise needs. All of which she would fulfill. It was the job she'd chosen because she took pride in her organizational skills, continually reordering her world throughout a chaotic childhood with an absentee father and a chronically ill mother. She took comfort in structuring what she could. And since there were only so many jobs on the island that could afford to pay her the kind of money she needed to support both her mother and her brother, Maresa had to succeed at the Carib Grand.

She calmed herself by squaring the single sheet of paper on her podium, lining up her pen beside it. She tapped open her list of restaurant phone numbers on her call screen so she could dial reservations at a moment's notice. The small, routine movements helped her to feel in control, reminding her she could do this job well. When she looked up again—

Wow.

The sight of the tall, chiseled male unfolding himself from the limousine was enough to take her breath away. His strong, striking features practically called for a feminine hand to caress them. Fraternizing with guests was, of course, strictly against the rules and Maresa had never been tempted. But if ever she had an inkling to stray from that philosophy, the powerful shoulders encased in expensive designer silk were exactly the sort of attribute that would intrigue her. The man towered over everyone in the courtyard entrance, including Big Bill, the head doorman. Dressed in a charcoal suit tailored to his long, athletic frame, the dark-haired guest buttoned his jacket, hiding too much of the hard, muscled chest that she'd glimpsed as he'd stepped out of the vehicle. Straightening his tie, he peered through the window, his ice-blue gaze somehow landing on her.

Direct hit.

She felt the jolt of awareness right through the glass. This supremely masculine specimen couldn't possibly be Mr. Holmes. Her brain didn't reconcile the image of a man with that square jaw and sharp blade of a nose ordering lilacs for himself. Daily.

Relaxing a fraction, Maresa blew out a breath as the newcomer turned back toward the vehicle. Until a silky white Maltese dog stepped regally from the limousine into the man's waiting arms.

In theory, Cameron McNeill liked dogs.

Big, slobbery working canines that thrived outdoors and could keep up with him on a distance run. The long-haired Maltese in his arms, on the other hand, was a prize-winning show animal with too many travel accessories to count. The retired purebred was on loan to Cam for his undercover assessment of a recently acquired McNeill Resorts property, however, and he needed Poppy's cooperation for his stint as a demanding hotel guest. If he walked into the financially floundering Carib Grand Hotel as himself—an owner and vice president of McNeill Resorts—he would receive the most attentive service imaginable and learn absolutely nothing about the establishment's underlying problems. But as Mr. Holmes, first-class pain in the ass, Cam would put the staff on their toes and see how they reacted.

After reviewing the Carib Grand's performance reports for the past two months, Cameron knew something was off in the day-to-day operations. And since he'd personally recommended that the company buy the property in the first place, he wasn't willing to wait for an over-priced operations review by an outside agency. Not that McNeill Resorts couldn't afford it. It simply chafed his pride that he'd missed something in his initial research. Besides, his family had just learned of a long-hidden branch of relations living on a nearby island—his father's sons by a secret mistress. Cam would use his time here to check out the other McNeills personally.

But for now? Business first.

"Welcome to the Carib Grand," an aging doorman greeted him with a deferential nod and a friendly smile.

Cam forced a frown onto his face to keep from smil-ing back. That wasn't as hard as he thought given the way Poppy's foolishly long fur was plastering itself to his jacket when he walked too fast, her topknot and tail bobbing with his stride and tickling his chin. It wouldn't come naturally to Cam to be the hard-to-please guest this week. He was a people-person to begin with, and appre-ciated those who worked for McNeill Resorts especially. But this was the fastest way he knew to find out what was going on at the hotel firsthand. He'd be damned if anyone on the board questioned his business acumen dur-ing a time when his aging grandfather was testing all his heirs for their commitment to his legacy.

The Carib Grand lobby was welcoming, as he recalled from his tour six months ago when the property had been briefly shut down. The two wings of the hotel flanked the reception area to either side with restaurants stacked overhead. But the lobby itself drew visitors in with floor-to-ceiling windows so the sparkling Caribbean beck-oned at all times. Huge hanging baskets of exotic flowers framed the view without impeding it.

The scent of bougainvillea drifted in through the door

behind him. Poppy tilted her nose in the air and took a seat on his forearm, a queen on her throne.

The front desk attendant—only one—was busy with another guest. Cameron's bellhop, a young guy with a long ponytail of dreadlocks, must have noticed the front desk was busy at the same time as him, because he gestured to the concierge's tall granite counter where a stunning brunette smiled.

"Ms. Delphine can help you check in, sir," the bellhop informed him while whisking his luggage onto a waiting cart. "Would you like me to walk the dog while you get settled?"

Nothing would please him more than to off-load Poppy and the miles of snow-white pet hair threading around his suit buttons. Cameron was pretty sure there was a cloud of fur floating just beneath his nose.

"Her name is Poppy," Cameron snapped at the helpful soul, unable to take his eyes off the very appealing concierge, who'd snagged his attention through the window the second he'd stepped out of the limo. "And I've requested a dog walker with references."

The bellhop gave a nod and backed away, no doubt glad to leave a surly guest in the hands of the bronze-skinned beauty sidling out from her counter to welcome Cameron. She seemed to have that mix of ethnicities common in the Caribbean. The burnished tint of her skin set off wide, tawny gold eyes. A natural curl and kink in her dusky brown hair ended in sun-blond tips. Perfect posture and a well-fitted linen suit made her look every inch a professional, yet her long legs drew his eye even though her skirt hit just above her knees. Even if he'd been visiting the property as her boss, he wouldn't have acted on the flash of attraction, of course. But it was a damn shame that he'd be at odds with this enticing female for the next two weeks. The concierge position was the linchpin in the hotel staff, though, and his mission to rattle cages began with her.

"Welcome, Mr. Holmes." He was impressed that she'd greeted him by name. "I'm Maresa. We're so glad to see you and Poppy, too."

He'd spoken to a Maresa Delphine on the phone earlier, purposely issuing a string of demands on short notice to see how she'd fare. She didn't look nervous. Yet. He'd need to challenge her, to prod at all facets of the management and staff to pinpoint the weak links. The hotel wasn't necessarily losing money, but it was only a matter of time before earnings followed the decline in performance reviews.

"Poppy will be glad to meet her walker." He came straight to the point, ignoring the eager bob of the dog's head as Maresa offered admiring words to the pooch. Cameron could imagine what the wag of the tail was doing to the back of his jacket. "Do you have the references ready?"

"Of course." Maresa straightened with a sunny smile. She had a hint of an accent he couldn't place. "They're right here at my desk."

Cameron's gaze dipped to her slim hips as she turned. He'd taken a hiatus from dating for fun over the last few months, thinking he ought to find himself a wife to fulfill his grandfather's dictate that McNeill Resorts would only go to the grandsons who were stable and wed. But he'd botched that, too, impulsively issuing a marriage proposal to the first woman his matchmaker suggested in order to have the business settled.

Now? Apparently the months without sex were conspiring against him. He ground his teeth against a surge of ill-timed desire.

"Here you go." The concierge turned with a sheet of paper in hand and passed it to him, her honey-colored gaze as potent as any caress. "I took the liberty of checking all the references myself, but I've included the numbers in case you'd like to talk to any of them directly."

"That's why I asked," he replied tightly, tugging the paper harder than necessary.

He could have sworn Poppy slanted him a dirty look over one fluffy white shoulder. Her nails definitely flexed into his forearm right through the sleeve of his suit before she fixed her coal-black eyes on Maresa Delphine.

Not that he blamed Poppy. He'd rather be staring at Maresa than scowling over dog walker references. Being the boss wasn't always a rocking-good time. Yet he'd rather ruffle feathers today and fix the core problems than have the staff jump though the hoops of an extended performance review.

Cameron slid the paper into his jacket pocket. "I'll check these after I have the chance to clean up. If you can have someone show us to our room."

He hurried her on purpose, curious if the room extras were ready to go. The bath wasn't a tough request, but the flowers had most likely needed to be flown in. If he hadn't been specifically looking for it, he might have missed the smallest hesitation on her part.

"Certainly." She lifted a tablet from the granite countertop where she worked. "If you can just sign here to approve the information you provided over the phone, I'll escort you myself."

That wasn't protocol. Did Ms. Delphine expect additional tips this way? Cam remembered reading that the concierge had been with the company since the reopening under McNeill ownership two months ago.

Signing his fake name on the electronic screen, he fished for information. "Are you understaffed?"

She ran a pair of keycards through the machine and slid them into a small welcome folder.

"Definitely not. We'll have Rudolfo bring your bags. I just want to personally ensure the suite is to your liking." She handed him the packet with the keys while giving a nod to the bell captain. "Can I make a dinner reservation for you this evening, Mr. Holmes?"

Cameron juggled the restless dog, who was no doubt more travel-weary than him. They'd taken a private jet, but even with the shorter air time, there'd been limo rides to and from airports, plus a boat crossing from Charlotte Amalie to the Carib Grand since the hotel occupied a small, private island just outside the harbor area in Saint Thomas. He'd walked the dog when they hit the ground at the airfield, but Poppy's owner had cautioned him to give the animal a certain amount of rest and play each day. So far on Cam's watch, Poppy had clocked zero time spent on both counts. For a pampered show dog, she was proving a trouper.

As soon as he banished the hotel staff including Maresa Delphine, he'd find a quiet spot on the beach where he and his borrowed pet could recharge.

"I've heard a retired chef from Paris opened a new restaurant in Martinique." He would be spending some time on that island where his half brothers were living. "I'd like a standing reservation for the rest of the week." He had no idea if he'd be able to get over there, but it was the kind of thing a good concierge could accommodate.

"I've heard La Belle Palm is fantastic." Maresa punched a button on the guest elevator while Rudolfo disappeared down another hall with the luggage. "I haven't visited yet, but I enjoyed Chef Pierre's La Luce on the Left Bank."

Her words brought to mind her résumé that he'd reviewed briefly before making the trip. She'd worked at a Paris hotel prior to accepting her current position.

"You've spent time in Paris, Ms. Delphine?" He set Poppy on the floor, unfurling the pink jeweled leash that had matched the carrying case Mrs. Trager had given him. He'd kept all the accessories except for that one— the huge pink pet carrier made Cam look like he was travelling with Barbie's Dreamhouse under his arm.

"She's so cute." Maresa kept her eyes on the dog and not on him. "And yes, I lived in Paris for a year before returning to Saint Thomas."

"You're from the area originally?" He almost regretted setting the dog down since it removed a barrier between them. Something about Maresa Delphine drew him in.

His gaze settled on the bare arch of her neck just above her jacket collar. Her thick brown hair had been clipped at the nape, ending in a silky tail that curled along one shoulder. A single pearl drop earring rolled along the tender expanse of skin, a pale contrast to her rich brown complexion.

"I grew up in Charlotte Amalie and worked in a local hotel until a foreign exchange program run by the corporate owner afforded me the chance to work overseas." She glanced up at him. Caught him staring.

The jolt of awareness flared, hot and unmistakable. He could tell she felt it, too. Her pupils dilated a fraction, dark pools with golden rims. His heartbeat slugged heavier. Harder.

He forced his gaze away as the elevator chimed to announce their arrival on his floor. "After you."

He held the door as she stepped out into the short hall.

They passed a uniformed attendant with a gallon-sized jug stuffed under his arm, a pair of earbuds half-in and half-out of his ears. After a quick glance at Maresa, the young man pulled the buds off and jammed them in his pocket, then shoved open a door to the stairwell.

"Here we are." Maresa stepped aside so Cam stood directly in front of the entrance to the Antilles Suite.

Poppy took a seat and stared at the door expectantly.

Cameron used the keycard to unlock the suite, not sure what to expect. Was Maresa Delphine worthy of what the company compensated her? Or had she returned to her hometown in order to bilk guests out of extra tips and take advantage of her employer? But she didn't appear to be looking for a bonus gratuity as her gaze darted around the suite interior and then landed on him.

Poppy spotted the patch of natural grass just outside the bathroom door. The sod rested inside a pallet on carpeted wheels, the cart painted in blues and tans to match the room's decorating scheme. The dog made a break for it and Cam let her go, the leash dangling behind her.

Lilacs flanked the crystal decanters on the minibar. Through the open door to the bathroom, Cameron could see the bubbles nearing the edge of the tub, the hot water still running as steam wafted upward.

So far, Maresa had proven a worthy concierge. That was good for the hotel, but less favorable for him, perhaps, since her high standards surely precluded acting on a fleeting elevator attraction.

"If everything is to your satisfaction, Mr. Holmes, I'll leave you undisturbed while I go make your dinner reservations for the week." She hadn't even allowed the door to close behind them, a wise practice, of course, for a female hotel employee.

Rudolfo was already in the hall with the luggage cart.

Cameron could hear Maresa giving the bellhop instructions for his bags. And Poppy's.

"Thank you." Cameron turned his back on her to stare out at the view of the hotel's private beach and the brilliant turquoise Caribbean Sea. "For now, I'm satisfied."

The room, of course, was fine. Ms. Delphine had passed his first test. But was he satisfied? No. He wouldn't rest until he knew why the guest reviews of the Carib Grand were lower than anticipated. And satisfaction was the last thing he was feeling when the most enticing woman he'd met in a long time was off-limits.

That attraction would be difficult to ignore when it was imperative he uncover all her secrets.

Two

As much as Maresa cursed her alarm clock chirping at her before dawn, she never regretted waking up early once she was on the Carib Grand's private beach before sunrise. Her mother's house was perched on a street high above Saint Thomas Harbor, which meant Maresa took a bike to the ferry each morning to get to the hotel property early for these two precious hours of alone time before work. Her brother was comfortable walking down to the dock later for his shift, a task that was overseen by a neighbor and fellow employee who also took the ferry over each day.

Now, rolling out her yoga mat on the damp sand, she made herself comfortable in child's pose, letting the magic of the sea and the surf do their work on her muscles tight with stress.

One. Two. Three. Breathe.

Smoothing her hands over the soft cotton of her bright

pink crop top, she felt her diaphragm lift and expand. She rarely saw anyone else on the beach at this hour, and the few runners or walkers who passed by were too busy soaking up the same quiet moments as she to pay her any mind.

Maresa counted through the inhales and exhales, trying her damnedest to let go of her worries. Too bad Cameron Holmes's ice-blue eyes and sculpted features kept appearing in her mind, distracting her with memories of that electric current she'd experienced just looking at him.

It made no sense, she lectured herself as she swapped positions for her sun salutations. The guest was demanding and borderline rude—something that shouldn't attract her in the slightest. She hated to think his raw masculinity was sliding under her radar despite what her brain knew about him.

At least she'd made it through the first day of his stay without incident. But while that was something to celebrate, she didn't want her brother crossing paths with the surly guest again. She'd held her breath yesterday when the two passed one another in the corridor outside the Antilles Suite, knowing how much Rafe loved dogs. Thankfully, her brother had been engrossed in his music and hadn't noticed the Maltese.

She'd keep Rafe safely away from Mr. Holmes for the next two weeks. Tilting her face to the soft glow of first light, she arched her back in the upward salute before sweeping down into a forward bend. Breathing out the challenges—living in tight quarters with her family, battling local agencies to get her brother into support programs he needed for his recovery, avoiding her former fiancé who'd texted her twice in the last twenty-four hours asking to see her— Maresa took comfort in this moment every day.

Shifting into her lunge as the sun peeked above the horizon, Maresa heard a dog bark before a small white ball of fluff careened past her toward the water. Startled by the sudden brush of fur against her arm, she had to reposition her hands to maintain her balance.

"Poppy." A man's voice sounded from somewhere in the woods behind the beach.

Cameron Holmes.

Maresa recognized the deep baritone, not by sound so much as by the effect it had on her. A slow, warm wave through the pit of her belly. What was the matter with her? She scrambled to her feet, realizing the pampered pet of her most difficult guest was charging into the Caribbean, happily chasing a tern.

"Poppy!" she called after the dog just as Cameron Holmes stepped onto the beach.

Shirtless.

She had to swallow hard before she lifted her fingers to her lips and whistled. The little Maltese stopped in the surf, peering back in search of the noise while the tern flew away up the shore. The ends of Poppy's glossy coat floated on the surface of the incoming tide.

The man charged toward his pet, his bare feet leaving wet footprints in the sand. Maresa was grateful for the moment to indulge her curiosity about him without his seeing her. A pair of bright board shorts rode low on his hips. The fiery glow of sunrise burnished his skin to a deeper tan, his square shoulders rolling with an easy grace as he scooped the animal out of the water and into his arms. He spoke softly to her even as the strands of long, wet fur clung to his side. Whatever he said earned him a heartfelt lick on the cheek from the pooch, its white tail wagging slowly.

Maresa's heart melted a little. Especially when she

caught a glimpse of Cameron Holmes's smile as he turned back toward her. For a moment, he looked like another man entirely.

Then, catching sight of her standing beside her yoga mat, his expression grew shuttered.

"Sorry to interrupt your morning." He gave a brief nod. Curt. Dismissive. "I thought the beach would be empty at this hour or I wouldn't have let her off the leash." He clipped a length of pink leather to the collar around Poppy's neck.

"Most days, I'm the only one down here at this time." She forced a politeness she didn't feel, especially when she wasn't on duty yet. "Would you like a towel for her?"

The animal wasn't shivering, but Maresa couldn't imagine it would be easy to groom the dog if she walked home with wet fur dragging on the ground.

"I didn't think to bring one with me." He frowned, glancing around the deserted beach as if one might appear. "I assumed towels would be provided."

She tried not to grind her teeth at the air of entitlement. It became far easier to ignore the appeal of his shirtless chest once he started speaking in that superior air.

"Towels are available when the beach cabana opens at eight." Bending to retrieve the duffel on the corner of her mat, she tugged out hers and handed it to him. "Poppy can have mine."

He hesitated.

She fought the urge to cram the terry cloth back in her bag and stomp off. But, of course, she couldn't do that. She reached toward the pup's neck and scratched her there instead. Poppy's heart-shaped collar jangled softly against Maresa's hand. She noticed the "If Found" name on the back.

Olivia Trager?

Maybe the animal belonged to a girlfriend.

"Thank you." He took the hand towel and tucked it around the dog. Poppy stared out of her wrap as if used to being swaddled. "I really didn't mean to interrupt you."

He sounded more sincere this time. Maresa glanced up at him, only to realize how close they were standing. His gaze roamed over her as if he had been taking advantage of an unseen moment, the same way she had ogled him earlier. Becoming aware of her skimpy yoga crop top and the heat of awareness warming her skin, she stepped back awkwardly.

"Ms. Trager must really trust you with her dog." She hadn't meant to say it aloud. Then again, maybe hearing about his girlfriend would stop these wayward thoughts about him. "That is, no wonder you want to take such good care of her."

Awkward much? Maresa cursed herself for sticking her nose in his personal business.

His expression remained inscrutable for a moment. He studied her as if weighing how much to share. "My mother wouldn't trust anyone but me with her dog," he said finally.

She considered his words, still half wishing the mystery Ms. Trager was a girlfriend on her way to the resort today. Then Maresa would have to take a giant mental step backward from the confusing hotel guest. As it stood, she had no one to save her from the attraction but herself. With that in mind, she raked up her yoga mat and started rolling it.

"Well, I hope the dog walker and groomer meet your criteria." She stuffed the mat in her duffel, wondering why he hadn't let the walker take the animal out in the first place. "I'm happy to find someone else if—"

"The walker is fine. You're doing an excellent job, Maresa."

The unexpected praise caught her off guard. She nearly dropped her bag, mostly because he fixed her with his clear blue gaze. Heat rushed through her again, and it didn't have anything to do with the sun bathing them in the morning light now that it was fully risen.

"Thank you." Her throat went dry. She backed up a step. Retreating. "I'm going to let you enjoy the beach."

Maresa turned toward the path through the thick undergrowth that led back to the hotel and nearly ran right into Jaden Torries, her ex-fiancé.

"Whoa!" Jaden's one hand reached to steady her, his other curved protectively around a pink bundle he carried. Tall and rangy, her artist ex-boyfriend was thin where Cameron was well-muscled. The round glasses Jaden wore for affectation and not because he needed them were jammed into the thick curls that reached his shoulders. "Maresa. I've been trying to contact you."

He released her, juggling his hold on the small pink parcel he carried. A parcel that wriggled?

"I've been busy." She wanted to pivot away from the man who'd told the whole island he was dumping her before informing her of the fact. But that shifting pink blanket captured her full attention.

A tiny wrinkled hand reached up from the lightweight cotton, the movement followed by the softest sigh imaginable.

Her ex-fiancé was carrying a baby.

"But this is important, Maresa. It's about Isla." He lowered his arm cradling the infant so Maresa could see her better.

Indigo eyes blinked up at her. Short dark hair complimented the baby's medium skin tone. A white cotton headband decorated with rosettes rested above barely there eyebrows. Perfectly formed tiny features were molded into a silent yawn, the tiny hands reaching heavenward as the baby shifted against Jaden.

Something shifted inside Maresa at the same time. A maternal urge she hadn't known she possessed seized her insides and squeezed tight. Once upon a time she had dreamed about having this man's babies. She'd imagined what they would look like. Now, he had sought her out to…taunt her with the life she'd missed out on?

The maternal urge hardened into resentment, but she'd be damned if she'd let him see it.

"Congratulations. Your daughter is lovely, Jaden." She straightened as the large shadow of Cameron Holmes covered them both.

"Is there a problem, Ms. Delphine?" His tone was cool and impersonal, yet in that awkward moment he felt like an ally.

She appreciated his strong presence beside her when she felt that old surge of betrayal. She let Jaden answer since she didn't feel any need to defend the ex who'd called off their wedding via a text message.

"There's no problem. I'm an old friend of Maresa's. Jaden Torries." He extended his free hand to introduce himself.

Mr. Holmes ignored it. Poppy barked at Jaden.

"Then I'm sure you'll respect Maresa's wish to be on her way." Her unlikely rescuer tucked his hand under one arm as easily as he'd plucked his pet from the water earlier.

The warmth of his skin made her want to curl into him just like Poppy had, too.

"Right." Jaden dropped his hand. "Except Rafe's old girlfriend, Trina, left town last night, Maresa. And since

Trina's my cousin, she stuck me with the job of delivering Rafe's daughter into your care."

Maresa's feet froze to the spot. She had a vague sense of Cameron leaning closer to her, his hand suddenly at her back. Which was helpful, because she thought for a minute there was a very real chance she was going to faint. Her knees wobbled beneath her.

"Sorry to spring it on you like this," Jaden continued. "I tried telling Trina she owed it to your family to tell you in person, and I thought I had her talked into it, but—"

"Rafe?" Maresa turned around slowly, needing to see with her own eyes if there was any chance Jaden was telling the truth. "Trina broke up with him almost a year ago. Right after the accident."

Jaden stepped closer. "Right. And Trina didn't even find out she was pregnant until a couple of weeks afterward, while Rafe was still in critical condition. Trina decided to go through with the pregnancy on her own. Isla was born the end of January."

Maresa was too shaken to even do the math, but she did know that Trina and Rafe had been hot and heavy for the last month or two they were together. They'd been a constant fixture on Maresa's social media feed for those weeks. Which had made it all the more upsetting when Trina bailed on him right after the accident, bursting into tears every time she got close to his bedside before giving up altogether. Had she been even more emotional because she'd been in the early stages of pregnancy?

"Why wouldn't she have called me or my mother?" Her knees wobbled again as her gaze fell on the tiny infant. Isla? She had Rafe's hairline—the curve of dark hair encroaching on the temples. But plenty of babies had that, didn't they? "I would have helped her. I could have been there when the baby was born."

"Who is Rafe?" Cameron asked.

She'd forgotten all about him.

Maresa gulped a breath. "My brother." The very real possibility that Jaden was telling the truth threatened to level her. Rafe was in no position to be a father with the assorted symptoms he still battled. And financially? She was barely getting by supporting her family and paying some of Rafe's staggering medical bills since he hadn't been fully insured at the time.

"Look." Jaden set a bright pink diaper bag down on the beach. Cartoon cats cartwheeled across the front. "My apartment is no place for a baby. You know that, right? I just took her because Trina showed up last night, begging me for help. I told her no, but told her she could spend the night. She took off while I was sleeping. But she left a note for you." He looked as though he wanted to sort through the diaper bag to find it, but before he leaned down he held the baby out to Maresa. "Here. Take her."

Maresa wasn't even sure she'd made up her mind to do so when Jaden thrust the warm, precious weight into her arms. He was still talking about Trina seeming "unstable" ever since giving birth, but Maresa couldn't follow his words with an infant in her arms. She felt stiff and awkward, but she was careful to support the squirming bundle, cradling the baby against her chest while Isla gurgled and kicked.

Maresa's heart turned over. Melted.

Here, the junglelike landscaping blocked out the sun where the tree branches arced over the dirt path. The scent of green and growing things mingled with the sea breeze and a hint of baby shampoo.

"She's a beauty," Cameron observed over her shoulder. He had set Poppy on the ground so he could get closer to Isla and Maresa. "Are you okay holding her?"

"Fine," she said automatically, not wanting to give her up. "Just...um...overwhelmed."

Glancing up at him, she caught her breath at the expression on his face as he looked down at the child in her arms. She had thought he seemed different—kinder—toward Poppy. But that unguarded smile she'd seen for the Maltese was nothing compared to the warmth in his expression as he peered down at the baby.

If she didn't know better—if she hadn't seen him be rude and abrupt with perfectly nice hotel staffers—she would have guessed she caught him making silly faces at Isla. The little girl appeared thoroughly captivated.

"Here it is." Jaden straightened, a piece of paper in his hand. "She left this for you along with some notes about the kid's schedule." He passed the papers to Cameron. "I've got to get going if I'm going to catch that ferry, Maresa. I only came out here because Trina gave me no choice, but I've got to get to work—"

"Seriously?" She had to work, too. But even as she was about to say as much, another voice in her head piped up. If Isla was really Rafe's child, would she honestly want Jaden Torries in charge of the baby for another minute? The answer was a crystal clear *absolutely not*.

"Drop her off at social services if you don't believe me." Jaden shrugged. "I've got a rich old lady client paying a whole hell of a lot for me to paint her portrait at eight." He checked his watch. "I'm outta here."

And with that, her ex-fiancé walked away, his sandy-gold curls bouncing. Poppy barked again, clearly unimpressed.

Social services? Really?

"If only I had Poppy around three years ago when I got engaged to him," she muttered darkly, hugging the baby tighter.

Cameron's hand briefly found the small of her back as he watched the other man leave. He clutched the letter from Rafe's former girlfriend—Isla's mother.

"And yet you didn't go through with the wedding. So you did just fine on your own." Cameron glanced down at her, his hand lingering on her back for one heart-stopping moment before it drifted away again. "Want me to read the letter? Or would you like me to take Isla so you can do the honors?"

He held the paper out for her to decide.

She liked him better here—outside the hotel. He was less intimidating, for one thing.

For another? He was appealing to her in all the ways a man could. A dangerous feeling for her when she needed to be on her guard around him. He was a guest, for crying out loud. But she was out of her depth with this precious little girl in her arms and she didn't know what she'd do if Cameron Holmes walked away from her right now. Having him there made her feel—if only for a moment—that she wasn't totally alone.

"Actually, I'd be really grateful if you would read it." She shook her head, tightening her hold on Isla. "I'm too nervous."

Katrina—Trina—Blanchett had been Rafe's girlfriend for about six months before the car accident. Maresa had never seen them together except for photos on social media of the two of them out playing on the beach or at the clubs. They'd seemed happy enough, but Rafe had told her on the phone it wasn't serious. The night of the accident, in fact, the couple had gotten into an argument at a bar and Trina had stranded him there. Rafe had called their mother for a ride, something she'd been only too happy to provide even though it was late. She'd never had an MS attack while driving before.

Less than ten days after seeing Rafe in the hospital, Trina had told Maresa through tears that she couldn't stand seeing him that way and it would be better for her to leave. At the time, Maresa had been too focused on Rafe's prognosis to worry about his flighty girlfriend. If she'd taken more time to talk to the girl, might she have confided the pregnancy news that followed the breakup?

"Would you like to have a seat?" Cameron pointed toward a bench near the outdoor faucet where guests could rinse off their feet. "You look too pale."

She nodded, certain she was pale. What was her mother going to say when she found out Rafe had a daughter? If he had a daughter. And Rafe? She couldn't imagine how frustrated he would feel to have been left out of the whole experience. Then again, how frustrated would he feel knowing that he couldn't care for his daughter the way he could have at one time?

Struggling to get her spinning thoughts under control, she allowed Cameron to guide her to the bench. Carefully, she lowered herself to sit with Isla, the baby blanket covering her lap since the kicking little girl had mostly freed herself of the swaddling. While she settled the baby, she noticed Cameron lift Poppy and towel her off a bit more before setting her down again. He double-checked the leash clip on her collar then took the seat beside Maresa.

"I'm ready," she announced, needing to hear whatever Isla's mother had to say.

Cameron unfolded the paper and read aloud. "'Isla is Rafe's daughter. I wasn't with anyone else while we were together. I was afraid to tell him about her after the doctor said he'd be...'" Cameron hesitated for only a moment "'...brain damaged. I know Rafe can't take care of her, but his mother will love her, right? I can't do this. I'm going to see my dad in Florida for a few weeks, but I'll sign papers to give you custody. I'm sorry."

Maresa listened to the silence following the words, her brain uncomprehending. How could the woman just take off and leave her baby—Rafe's baby—with Jaden Torries while she traveled to Florida? Who did that? Trina wasn't a kid—she was twenty-one when she'd dated Rafe. But she'd never had much family support, according to Rafe. Her mother was an alcoholic and her father had raised her, but he'd never paid her much attention.

A fierce surge of protectiveness swelled inside of Maresa. It was so strong she didn't know where to put it all. But she knew for damn sure that she would protect little Isla—her niece—far better than the child's mother had. And she would call a lawyer and find out how to file for full custody.

"You could order DNA testing," Cameron observed, his impressive abs rippling as he leaned forward on the bench. "If you are concerned she's not a biological relative."

Maresa closed her eyes for a moment to banish all thoughts of male abs, no matter how much she welcomed the distraction from the monumental life shift taking place for her this morning.

"I'll ask an attorney about it when I call to find out how I can secure legal custody." She wrapped Isla's foot back in a corner of the blanket. "For right now, I need to find suitable care for Isla before my shift at the Carib begins for the day." Throat burning, Maresa realized she was near tears just thinking about the unfairness of it all. Not to *her*, of course, because she would make it work no matter what life threw at her.

But how unfair to *Rafe*, who wouldn't be able to parent his child without massive amounts of help. Perhaps he wouldn't be interested in parenting at all. Would he be angry? Would Trina's surprise be the kind of thing that unsettled his confused mind and set back his recovery?

She would call his counselor before saying anything to him. That call would be right after she spoke to a lawyer. She wasn't even ready to tell her mother yet. Analise Delphine's health was fragile and stress could aggravate it. Maresa wanted to be sure she was calm before she spoke to her mother. They'd all been in the dark for months about Trina's pregnancy. A few more hours wouldn't matter one way or another.

"I noticed on the dog walker's résumé that she has experience working in a day care." Cameron folded the paper from Trina and inserted it into an exterior pocket of the diaper bag. "And as it happens, I already walked the dog. Would you like me to text her and ask her to meet you somewhere in the hotel to give you a hand?"

Maresa couldn't imagine what that would cost. But what were her options since she didn't want to upset her mother? She didn't have time to return home and give the baby to her mother even if she was sure her mother could handle the shocking news.

"That would be a great help, thank you. The caregiver can meet me in the women's locker room by the pool in twenty minutes." Shooting to her feet, Maresa realized she'd imposed on Cameron Holmes's kindness for far too long. "And with that, I'll let you and Poppy get back to your morning walk."

"I'll go with you. I can carry the baby gear." He reached for the pink diaper bag, but she beat him to it.

"I'm fine. I insist." She pasted on her best concierge smile and tried not to think about how comforting it had felt to have him by her side this morning. Now more than ever, she needed job security, which meant she couldn't let an important guest think she made a habit of bringing her personal life to work. "Enjoy your day, Mr. Holmes."

Enjoying his day proved impossible with visions of Maresa Delphine's pale face circling around Cameron's head the rest of the morning. He worked at his laptop on the private terrace off his room, distracted as hell thinking about the beautiful, efficient concierge caught off guard by a surprise that would have damn near leveled anyone else.

She'd inherited her brother's baby. A brother who, from the sounds of it, was not in any condition to care for his child himself.

Sunlight glinted off the sea and the sounds from the beach floated up to his balcony. The noises had grown throughout the morning from a few circling gulls to the handful of vacationing families that now populated the beach. The scent of coconut sunscreen and dense floral vegetation swirled on the breeze. But the temptation of a tropical paradise didn't distract Cam from his work nearly as much as memories of his morning with Maresa.

Shocking encounter with the baby aside, he would still have been distracted just remembering her limber arched back, her beautiful curves outlined by the light of the rising sun when he'd first broken through the dense undergrowth to find her on the private beach. Her skimpy workout gear had skimmed her hips and breasts, still tantalizing the hell out of him when he was supposed to be researching the operations hierarchy of the Carib Grand on his laptop.

But then, all that misplaced attraction got funneled into protectiveness when he'd met her sketchy former fiancé. He'd met the type before—charming enough, but completely self-serving. The guy couldn't have come up with a kinder way to inform her of her niece's existence?

On the plus side, Cameron had located some search results about her brother. Rafe Delphine had worked at the hotel for one month in a hire that some might view as unethical given his relationship to Maresa. But his application—though light on work history—had been approved by the hotel director on-site, so the young man must be fit for the job despite his injury in a car wreck the year before. That, too, had been an easy internet search, with local news articles reporting the crash and a couple of updates on Rafe's condition afterward. The trauma the guy had suffered must have been harrowing for his whole family. Clearly the girlfriend had found it too much to handle.

Now, as a runner for the concierge, Rafe would be directly under Maresa's supervision. That concerned Cameron since Maresa would have every reason in the world to keep him employed. As much as Cam empathized with her situation—all the more now that she'd discovered her brother had an heir—he couldn't afford to ignore good business practices. He'd have to speak to the hotel director about the situation and see if they should make a change.

The ex-fiancé was next on his list of searches. Not that he wanted to pry into Maresa's private life. Cameron was more interested in seeing how the guy connected to the Carib Grand that he'd come all the way to the hotel's private island to pass over the baby. That seemed like an unnecessary trip unless he was staying here or worked here. Why not just give the baby to Maresa at her home in Charlotte Amalie? Why come to her place of work when it was so far out of the way?

Cam had skimmed halfway through the short search results on Jaden Torries's portraits of people and pets before his phone buzzed with an incoming call. Poppy, snoozing in the shade of the chair under his propped feet, didn't even stir at the sound. The dog was definitely making up for lost rest from the day before.

Glimpsing his oldest brother's private number, Cam hit the button to connect the call. "Talk to me."

"Hello to you, too." Quinn's voice came through along with the sounds of Manhattan in the background—horns honking, brakes squealing, a shrill whistle and a few shouts above the hum of humanity indicating he must be on the street. "I wanted to give you a heads-up I just bought a sea plane."

"Nice, bro, But there's no way you'll get clearance to land in the Hudson with that thing." Cameron scrolled to a gallery of Torries's work and was decidedly unimpressed.

Not that he was an expert. But as a supporter of the arts in Manhattan for all his adult life, he felt reasonably sure Maresa's ex was a poser. Then again, maybe he just didn't like a guy who'd once commanded the concierge's attention.

"The aircraft isn't for me," Quinn informed him. "It's for you. I figured it would be easier than a chopper to get from one island to another while you're investigating the Carib Grand and checking out the relatives."

Cam shoved aside his laptop and straightened. "Seriously? You bought a seaplane for my two-week stay?"

As a McNeill, he'd grown up with wealth, yes. He'd even expanded his holdings with the success of the gaming development company he'd started in college. But damn. He limited himself to spending within reason.

"The Carib Grand is the start of our Caribbean expansion, and if it goes well, we'll be spending a lot of time and effort developing the McNeill brand in the islands and South America. We have a plane available in the Mediterranean. Why not keep something accessible on this side of the Atlantic?"

"Right." Cam's jaw flexed at the thought of how much was riding on smoothing things out at the Carib Grand. A poor bottom line wasn't going to help the expansion program. "Good thinking."

"Besides, I have the feeling we'll be seeing our half brothers in Martinique a whole lot more now that Gramps is determined to bring them into the fold." Quinn sounded as grim about that prospect as Cameron felt. "So the plane might be useful for all of us as we try to…contain the situation."

Quinn wanted to keep their half siblings out of Manhattan and out of the family business as much as Cameron did. They'd worked too hard to hand over their company to people who'd never lifted a finger to grow McNeill Resorts.

"Ah." Cam stood to stretch his legs, surprised to realize it was almost noon according to the slim dive watch he'd worn for his morning laps. "But since I'm on the front line meeting them, I'm going to leave it up to you or Ian to be the diplomatic peacemakers."

Quinn only half smothered a laugh. "No one expected you of all people to be the diplomat. Dad's still recovering from the punch you gave him last week when he dropped the I-have-another-family bombshell on us."

Definitely not one of his finer moments. "It seemed like he could have broached the topic with some more tact."

"No kidding. I kept waiting for Sofia to break the engagement after the latest family soap opera." The background noise on Quinn's call faded. "Look, Cam, I just arrived at Lincoln Center to take her out to lunch. I'll text you the contact details for a local pilot."

Cam grinned at the thought of his stodgy older brother

so head over heels for his ballerina fiancée. The same ballerina fiancée Cam had impulsively proposed to last winter when a matchmaker set them up. But even if Cam and Sofia hadn't worked out, the meeting had been a stroke of luck for Quinn, who'd promptly stepped in to woo the dancer.

"Thanks. And give our girl a kiss from me, okay?" It was too fun to resist needling Quinn. Especially since Cameron was two thousand miles away from a retaliatory beat-down.

A string of curses peppered his ear before Quinn growled, "It's not too late to take the plane back."

"Sorry." Cameron wasn't sorry. He was genuinely happy for his brother. "I'll let you know if the faux McNeills are every bit as awful as we imagine."

Disconnecting the call, Cameron texted a message to the dog groomer to give Poppy some primp time. He'd use that window of freedom to follow up on a few leads around the Carib Grand. He wanted to find out what the hotel director thought about Rafe Delphine, for one thing. The director was the only person on-site who knew Cameron's true identity and mission at the hotel. Aldo Ricci had been successful at McNeill properties in the Mediterranean and Malcolm McNeill had personally appointed the guy to make the expansion program a success.

With the McNeill patriarch's health so uncertain, Cameron wanted to respect his grandfather's choices. All the more so since he still hadn't married the way his granddad wanted.

Cameron would start by speaking to his grandfather's personally chosen manager. Cam had a lot of questions about the day-to-day operations and a few key personnel. Most especially the hotel's new concierge, who kept too many secrets behind her beautiful and efficient facade.

Three

Seated in the hotel director's office shortly after noon, Cameron listened to Aldo Ricci discuss his plans for making the Carib Grand more profitable over the next two quarters. Unlike Cameron, the celebrated hotel director with a crammed résumé of successes did not seem concerned about the dip in the Carib Grand's performance.

"All perfectly normal," the impeccably dressed director insisted, prowling around his lavish office on the ground floor of the property. A collector of investment-grade wines, Aldo incorporated a few rare vintages into his office decor. A Bordeaux from Moulin de La Lagune rested casually on a shelf beside some antique corkscrews and a framed invitation from a private tasting at Château Grand Corbin. "We are only beginning to notice the minute fluctuations now that our capacity for data is greater than ever. But those irregularities will not even be noticeable by the time we hit our performance and profit goals for the end of the year."

The heavyset man tugged on his perfectly straight suit cuffs. The fanciness of the dark silk jacket he wore reminded Cameron how many times the guy had taken a property out of the red and into the ranks of the most prestigious places in the world. To have enticed him to McNeill Resorts had been a coup, according to Cameron's grandfather.

"Nevertheless, I'd like to know more about Maresa Delphine." Cameron didn't reveal his reasons. He could see her now through the blinds in the director's office. She strode along the pool patio outside, hurrying past the patrons in her creamy linen blazer with an orchid at the lapel. Her sun-splashed brown hair gleamed in the bright light, but something about her posture conveyed her tension. Worry.

Was she thinking about Isla?

He made a mental note to check on the sitter and be sure she was doing a good job with the baby. Little Isla had tugged at his heartstrings this morning with her tiny, restless hands and her expressive face. That feeling—the warmth for the baby—shocked him. Not that he was an ogre or anything, but he'd decided long ago not to have kids of his own.

He was too much like his father—impulsive, fun-loving, easily distracted—to be a parent. After all, Liam McNeill had turfed out responsibility for his sons at the first possible opportunity, letting the boys' grandfather raise them the moment Liam's Brazilian wife got tired of his globe-trotting, daredevil antics. Cameron had always known his father had shirked the biggest responsibility of his life and that, coupled with his own tendency to follow his own drummer, had been enough to convince Cam that kids weren't for him. And that had been before discovering his dad had fathered a whole other set of kids with someone else.

Before an accident that had compromised Cameron's ability to have a family anyhow.

"Maresa Delphine is a wonderful asset to the hotel," the director assured him, coming around to the front of his desk to sit beside Cameron in the leather club chairs facing the windows. "If you seek answers about the hotel workings, I urge you to reveal your identity to her. I know you want to remain incognito, but I assure you, Ms. Delphine is as discreet and professional as they come."

"Yet you've only known her for...what? Two months?"

"Far longer than that. She worked at another property in Saint Thomas where I supervised her three years ago. I personally recommended her to a five-star property in Paris because I was impressed with her work and she was eager to...escape her hometown for a while. I had no reservations about helping her win the spot. She makes her service her top priority." The director crossed one leg over the other and pointed to a crystal decanter on the low game table between them. "Are you sure I can't offer you anything to drink?"

"No. Thank you." He wanted a clear head for deciding his next move with Maresa. Revealing himself to her was tempting considering the attraction simmering just beneath the surface. But he couldn't forget about the gut instinct that told him she was hiding something. "What can you tell me about her brother?"

"Rafe is a fine young man. I would have gladly hired him even without Maresa's assurances she would watch over him."

"Why would she need to?" He was genuinely curious

about the extent of Rafe's condition. Not only because she seemed protective of him, but also because Maresa hadn't argued Trina's depiction of her brother as "brain damaged."

"Rafe has a traumatic brain injury. He's the reason Maresa gave up the job in Paris. She rushed home to take care of her family. The young man is much better now. Although he can become agitated or confused easily, he has good character, and we haven't put him in a position where he will have much contact with guests." Aldo smiled as he smoothed his tie. "Maresa feels a strong sense of responsibility for him. But I've seen no reason to regret hiring her sibling. She knows, however, that Rafe's employment is on a trial basis."

Aldo Ricci seemed like the kind of man to trust his gut, which might be fine for someone who'd been in the business for as long as he had, but Cameron still wondered if he was overlooking things.

Maybe he should confide in Maresa if only to discover her take on the staff at the Carib Grand. Specifically, he wondered, what was her impression of Aldo Ricci? Cameron found himself wanting to know a lot more about the operations of the hotel.

"Perhaps I will speak to Ms. Delphine." Cameron wanted to find her now, in fact. His need to see her has been growing ever since she'd walked away from him early that morning. "I'd like some concrete answers about those performance reviews, even if they do seem like minute fluctuations."

He rose from his seat, liking the new plan more than he should. *Damn it.* Spending more time with Maresa didn't mean anything was going to happen between them. As her boss, of course, he had a responsibility to ensure it didn't.

And, without question, she had a great deal on her

mind today of all days. But maybe that was all the more reason to give her a break from the concierge stand. Perhaps she'd welcome a few hours away from the demands of the guests.

"Certainly." The hotel director followed him to the door. "There's no one more well-versed in the hotel except for me." His grin revealed a mouth full of shiny white veneers. "Stick close to her."

Cameron planned to do just that.

"Have you seen Rafe?" Maresa asked Nancy, the waitress who worked in the lobby bar shortly after noon. "I wanted to eat lunch with him."

Standing beside Nancy, a tall blonde goddess of a woman who probably made more in tips each week than Maresa made in a month, she peered out over the smattering of guests enjoying cocktails and the view. Her brother was nowhere in sight.

She had checked on Isla a few moments ago, assuring herself the baby was fine. She'd shared Trina's notes about the baby's schedule with the caregiver, discovering Isla's birth certificate with the father's name left blank and a birth date of ten weeks prior. And after placing a call to Trina's mother, Maresa had obtained contact information for the girl's father in Florida, who'd been able to give her a number for Trina herself. The girl had tearfully confirmed everything she said in her note—promising to give custody of the child to Rafe's family since she wasn't ready to be a mother and she didn't trust her own mother to be a good guardian.

The young woman had been so distraught, Maresa had felt sorry for her. All the more so because Trina had tried to handle motherhood alone when she'd been so conflicted about having a baby in the first place.

Now, Maresa wanted to see Rafe for herself to make sure he was okay. What if Jaden had mentioned Isla to him? Or even just mentioned Trina leaving town? Rafe hadn't asked about his girlfriend since regaining consciousness. She suspected Rafe would have been walking onto the ferry that morning the same time as Jaden was walking off.

Earlier that day, she'd left him a to-do list when she'd had an appointment to keep with the on-site restaurant's chef. She'd given Rafe only two chores, and they were both jobs he'd done before so she didn't think he'd have any trouble. He had to pick up some supplies at the gift shop and deliver flowers to one of the guests' rooms.

"I saw him about an hour ago." Nancy rang out a customer's check. "He brought me this." She pointed to the tiny purple wildflowers stuffed behind the engraved silver pin with her name on it. "He really is the sweetest."

"Thank you for being so kind to him." Maresa had witnessed enough people be impatient and rude to him that he'd become her barometer for her measure of a person. People who were nice to Rafe earned her respect.

"Kind to *him*?" Nancy tossed her head back and laughed, her long ponytail swishing. "That boy should earn half my tips since it's Rafe who makes me smile when I feel like strangling some of my more demanding customers—like that Mr. Holmes." She straightened the purple blooms with one hand and shoved the cash drawer closed with her hip. "These flowers from your brother are the nicest flowers any man has ever given me."

Reassured for the moment, Maresa felt her heart squeeze at the words. Her brother had the capacity for great love despite the frustrations of his injury. Maybe he'd come to accept his daughter as part of his life down the road.

Until then, she needed to keep them both safely employed and earning benefits to take care of their family.

"It makes me happy to hear you say that." Maresa turned on her heel, leaving Nancy to her job. "If you see him, will you let him know I'm having lunch down by the croquet field?"

"Sure thing." Nancy lifted a tray full of drinks to take to another table. "Sometimes he hangs out in the break room if the Yankees are on the radio, you know. You might check if they play today."

"Okay. Thanks." She knew her brother liked listening to games on the radio. Being able to listen on his earbuds was always soothing for him.

Maresa hitched her knapsack with the insulated cooler onto her shoulder to carry out to the croquet area. The field didn't officially open again until late afternoon when it cooled down, so no one minded if employees sat under the palm trees there for lunch. There were a handful of places like that on the private island—spots where guests didn't venture that workers could enjoy. She needed a few minutes to collect herself. Come up with a plan for what she was going to do with a ten-week-old infant after work. And what she would tell Rafe about the baby since his counselor hadn't yet returned her phone call.

Her phone vibrated just then as her sandals slapped along the smooth stone path dotted with exotic plantings on both sides. Her mother's number filled the screen.

"Mom?" she answered quietly while passing behind the huge pool and cabanas that surrounded it. The area was busy with couples enjoying outdoor meals or having cocktails at the swim-up bar and families playing in the nearby surf. Seeing a mother share a bite of fresh pineapple with her little girl made Maresa's breath catch.

She'd once dreamed of being a mother to Jaden's children until he betrayed her.

Now, she might be a single mother to her brother's baby if Trina truly relinquished custody.

She scuttled deeper into the shade of some palms for her phone conversation, knowing she couldn't blurt out Isla's existence to her mom on the phone even though, in the days before her mother's health had taken a downhill spiral, she might have been tempted to do just that.

"No need to worry." Her mother's breathing sounded labored. From stress? Or exertion? She tired so easily over the past few months. "I just wanted to let you know your brother came home."

Maresa's steps faltered. Stopped.

"Rafe is there? With you?" Panic tightened her shoulders and clenched her gut. She peered around the path to the croquet field, half hoping her brother would come strolling toward her anyhow, juggling some pilfered deck cushions for her to sit on for an impromptu picnic the way he did sometimes.

"He showed up about ten minutes ago. I would have called sooner, but he was upset and I had to calm him down. I guess the florist gave him a pager—"

"Oh no." Already, Maresa could guess what had happened. "Those are really loud." The devices vibrated and blinked, setting off obnoxious alarms that would startle anyone, let alone someone with nervous tendencies. The floral delivery must not have been prepared when Rafe arrived to pick it up, so they gave him the pager to let him know when it was ready.

"He got scared and dropped it, but I'm not sure where—" Her mother stopped speaking, and in the background, Maresa heard Rafe shouting "I don't know, I don't know, I don't know" in a frightened chorus.

Her gut knotted. How could she bring a ten-week-old into their home tonight, knowing how loud noises upset her brother?

"Tell him everything's fine. I'll find the pager." Turning on her heel, she headed back toward the hotel. She thought the device turned itself off after a few minutes anyhow, but just in case it was still beeping, she'd rather find it before anyone else on staff. "I can probably retrace his steps since I sent him on those errands. I'll deliver the flowers myself."

"Honey, you're taking on too much having him there with you. You don't want to risk your job."

And the alternative? They didn't have one. Especially now with little Isla's care to consider.

"My job will be fine," she reassured her mother as she tugged open a door marked Employees Only that led to the staff room and corporate offices. She needed to sign Rafe out for the day before she did anything else.

Blinking against the loss of sunlight, Maresa felt the blast of air conditioning hit her skin, which had gone clammy with nervous sweat. She picked at the neckline of her thin silk camisole beneath her linen jacket.

"Ms. Delphine?" a familiar masculine voice called to her from the other end of the corridor.

Even before she turned, she knew who she would see. The tingling that tripped over her skin was an unsettling mix of anticipation and dread.

"Mom, I'll call you back." Disconnecting quickly, she dropped the phone in her purse and turned to see Cameron Holmes striding out of the hotel director's office, her boss at his side.

"Mr. Holmes." She forced a smile for both men, wondering why life was conspiring so hard against her today. What on earth would a guest be doing in the hotel director's office if not to complain? Unless maybe he had something extremely valuable he wanted to place in the hotel safe personally.

Highly unorthodox, but that's the only other reason she could think of to explain his presence here.

"Maresa." Her hotel director nodded briefly at her before shaking hands with Cameron Holmes. "And sir, I appreciate you coming to me directly. I certainly understand the need for discretion."

Aldo Ricci turned and re-entered his office, leaving Maresa with a racing heart in the presence of Cameron Holmes, who looked far more intimidating in a custom navy silk suit and a linen shirt open at the throat than he had in his board shorts this morning.

The level of appeal, however, seemed equal on both counts. She couldn't forget his unexpected kindness on the beach no matter how demanding he'd been as a hotel guest.

"Just the woman I was hoping to see." His even white teeth made a quick appearance in what passed for a smile. "Would you join me for a moment in the conference room?"

No.

Her brain filled in the answer even as her feet wisely followed where he led. She didn't want to be alone with him anywhere. Not when she entertained completely inappropriate thoughts about him. She couldn't let her attraction to a guest show.

Furthermore? She needed to sign her brother out of work, locate the pager he'd lost and deliver those flowers before the florist got annoyed and reported Rafe for not doing his job. Now was not the time for fantasizing about a wealthy guest who could afford to shape the world to his liking, even if he had the body of a professional surfer underneath that expensive suit.

As she crossed the threshold into the Carib Grand's private conference room full of tall leather chairs around an antique table, Maresa realized she couldn't do this. Not now.

"Actually, Mr. Holmes," she said, spinning around to face him and misjudging how close he followed behind her.

Suddenly, she stood nose-to-nose with him, her thigh grazing his, her breast brushing his strong arm. She stepped back fast, heat flooding her cheeks. The contact was so brief, she could almost tell herself it hadn't happened, except that her body hummed with awareness where they'd touched.

And then, there was the fact that he gripped her elbow when she wobbled.

"Sorry," she blurted, tugging away from him completely as the door to the conference room closed automatically behind them.

Sealing them in privacy.

Sunlight spilled in behind her, the Caribbean sun the only illumination in the room that hadn't been in use yet today. The quiet was deep here, the carpet muffling his step as he shifted closer.

"Are you all right?" His forehead creased with concern. "Are you comfortable with the caregiver for Isla?"

She glanced up at him, surprised at the thoughtful question. He really had been supportive this morning, giving her courage during an impossible situation. Right now, however, it was difficult to focus on his kind side when the man was simply far too handsome. She wished fervently he had that adorable little dog with him so she could pet Poppy instead of thinking about how hot Mr. Holmes could be when he wasn't scowling.

"I'm fine. I have everything under control." *Um, if*

only. Clearly, she needed to date more often so she didn't turn into a babbling idiot around handsome men during work hours. "It's just that you caught me on my lunch hour, so I'm not technically working."

"Unfortunately, Maresa, I am." He folded his arms across his chest before he paced halfway across the room.

Confused, she watched him. He was not an easy man to look away from.

"I don't understand." She wondered how it happened that being around him made her feel like there wasn't enough air in the room. Like she couldn't possibly catch her breath.

"I'm doing some work for the hotel," he explained, pacing back toward her. "Secretly."

Confusion filled her as she tried to sort through his words that didn't make a bit of sense.

"So you're not actually on vacation at all? What kind of work?" She could think better now that he was on the opposite side of the room. "Is that why you were in the hotel director's office?"

"Yes. My real name is Cameron McNeill and I'm investigating why guest satisfaction has been declining over the last two months." He kept coming toward her, his blue eyes zeroing in on her. "And now I'm beginning to think you're the only person who can help me figure out why."

Cameron could feel her nervousness as clearly as if it was his own.

She stood, alert and ready to flee, her tawny eyes wide. She bit her full lower lip.

"McNeill? As in McNeill Resorts?" She blinked slowly. "The same."

"Why do you think I can help you?" She smoothed the

cuff of her ivory-colored linen jacket and then swiped elegant fingers along her forehead as if perspiring in spite of the fact she looked cool. So incredibly smooth and cool.

He hated doing this to her today of all days. The woman had just found out her brother had a child who would—he suspected—become her financial and familial dependent. What he'd gathered about Rafe Delphine's health suggested the man wouldn't be in any position to care for a newborn, and Aldo Ricci had made it clear Maresa put her family before herself.

"Preliminary data indicates the Carib is floundering in performance reviews and customer satisfaction." That was true enough. "You have a unique perspective on the hotel and everyone who works here. I'd like to know your views on why that might be?"

"And my boss told you I would talk to you about those issues?" Her gaze flitted to the door behind him and then back to him as if she would rather be anywhere else than right here.

Truth be told, he was a little uncomfortable being alone with her under these circumstances himself. She was far too tempting to question in the privacy of an empty conference room when the attraction was like a live wire sending sparks in all directions.

How could he ignore that?

"Your hotel director assured me you would be discreet."

She'd garnered the respect of her peers. The praise of superiors. All of which only made Cameron more curious about her. He stopped in front of her. At a respectable distance. He held her gaze, not allowing his eyes to wander.

"Of course, Mr. McNeill." She fidgeted with a bracelet—a shiny silver star charm—partially hidden by the sleeve of her jacket. "But what exactly did he hope I could share with you?"

"Call me Cam. And I hope you will share any insights about the staff and even some of the guests." He knew the data could be skewed by one or two unhappy visitors, particularly if they were vocal about their displeasure with the hotel.

"A difficult line to walk considering how much a concierge needs to keep her guests happy. It doesn't serve me—or McNeill Resorts—to betray confidences of valued clients."

Cameron couldn't help the voice in his head that piped up just then, wanting to know what she might have done to keep *him* happy as her guest.

Focus, damn it.

"And yet, you'll want to please the management as well," he reminded her. "Correct?"

"Of course." She nodded, letting go of the silver star so the bracelet slipped lower on her wrist.

"So how about if I buy you lunch and we'll begin our work together? I'll speak to Mr. Ricci about giving you the afternoon off." He needed to take her somewhere else. A place where the temptation to touch her wouldn't get the better of him. "We can bring Isla."

Nothing stifled attraction like an infant, right?

"Thank you, Mr. Mc—er, Cam." Maresa's face lit up with a glow that damn near took his breath away; her relief and eagerness to be reunited with the little girl were all too obvious. "That would be really wonderful."

Her pleasure affected him far more than it should, making him wonder how he could make that smile return to her face again and again. Had he really thought a baby would dull his desire for Maresa?

Not a chance.

Four

"You rented a villa here," Maresa observed as she held the ends of her hair in one hand to keep it from flying away in the open-top Jeep Cameron McNeill used for tooling around the private island. "In addition to the hotel suite."

The Jeep bounced down a long road through the lush foliage to a remote part of the island. In theory, she knew about the private villas that the Carib Grand oversaw on the extensive property, but the guests who took those units had their own staff so she didn't see them often and she'd never toured them. She turned in her seat to peer back at Isla, in the car seat she'd procured from the hotel. The baby faced backward with a sunshade tilted over the seat, but Maresa could see the little girl was still snoozing contentedly.

The caregiver had fed and changed her, and before Maresa could compensate her, Cameron had taken care of the bill, insisting that he make the day as easy as possible for Maresa to make up for the inconvenience of working with him. Spending the day in a private villa with yet another caregiver—this one a licensed nurse from the hospital in Saint Thomas who would meet them there—was hardly an inconvenience. Truth be told, she was grateful to escape the hotel for the day after the stress of discovering Isla and finding out that Rafe had left work without authorization. Luckily, she'd signed him out due to illness and found the pager he dropped on her way to pick up Isla from the caregiver. Maresa had assigned the flower delivery to another runner before leaving.

Now, all she had to do was get through an afternoon with her billionaire boss who'd only been impersonating a pain-in-the-butt client. But what if Cameron McNeill turned out to be even more problematic than his predecessor, Mr. Holmes?

"The villas are managed by a slightly different branch of the company," Cameron informed her, using a remote to open a heavy wrought-iron gate that straddled the road ahead. "My privacy is protected here. I'll return to the hotel suite later tonight to continue my investigation work under Mr. Holmes's name. Unless, of course, you and I can figure out the reason behind the declining reviews before then."

The ocean breeze whipped another strand of Maresa's hair free from where she'd been holding it, the wavy lock tickling against her cheek and teasing along her lips. What was it about Cameron's physical presence that made her so very aware of her own? She'd never felt so on edge around Jaden even when they'd been wildly in love. Cameron's nearness made her feel...anxious. Expectant.

"From my vantage point, everything has been running smoothly at the Carib." Maresa didn't need a poor performance review. What if Cameron McNeill thought that the real reason for the declining ratings was her? A concierge could make or break a customer's experience of any hotel. Maybe this meeting with the boss wasn't to interview her so much as to interrogate her.

But damn it, she knew her performance had been exemplary.

"We'll figure it out, one way or another," Cameron assured her as the Jeep climbed a small hill and broke through a cluster of trees.

The most breathtaking view imaginable spread out before her. She gasped aloud.

"Oh wow." She shook her head at the sparkling expanse of water lapping against White Shoulders Beach below them. On the left, the villa sat at the cliff's edge, positioned so that the windows, balconies and infinity pool all faced the stunning view. "I grew up here, and still—you never grow immune to this."

"I can see why." He pulled the Jeep into a sheltered parking bay beside a simple silver Ford sedan. "It looks like the sitter has already arrived. We can get Isla settled inside with some air conditioning and then get to work."

Unfastening her gaze from the view of Saint John's in the distance, and a smattering of little islands closer by, Maresa turned to take in the villa. The Aerie was billed as the premiere private residence on the island; she thought she recalled the literature saying it was almost twenty thousand square feet. It was a palatial home decorated in the Mediterranean style. The white-sashed stucco and deep bronze roof tiles were an understated color combination, especially when accented with weathered gray doors. The landscaping dominated the home from the outside, but there were balconies everywhere to take advantage of the views.

Sliding out of the Jeep, she smoothed a hand over her windblown hair to try to prepare herself for what was no doubt the most important business meeting of her life. She couldn't allow her guard to slip, not even when Cameron McNeill spared a kind smile for Baby Isla as he carefully unbuckled her from the car seat straps.

"Need any help?" she asked, stepping closer to the Jeep again.

"I've got it." He frowned slightly, reaching beneath the baby to palm her head in his big hand. He supported her back with his forearm, cradling her carefully until he had her tucked against his chest. "There." He grinned over at Maresa. "Just like carrying a football. You take the fall yourself before you fumble."

"Ideally, there's no falling involved for anyone." She knew he was teasing, but she wondered if she should have offered to carry Isla just the same.

She couldn't deny she was a bit overwhelmed, though. She didn't know much about babies, and now she would be lobbying for primary custody of Rafe's little girl, even if Trina changed her mind. Maresa knew Rafe would have wanted to exercise his parental rights, and she would do that in his place. Still, it was almost too much to get her brain around in just a few hours, and she had no one she could share the news with outside of Rafe's counselor. Oddly, having Cameron McNeill beside her today had anchored her when she felt most unsteady, even as she knew she had to keep her guard up around him.

Half an hour later, Maresa finally managed to walk out of the makeshift nursery—a huge suite of rooms adapted for the purpose with the portable crib the hospital nurse had brought with her. The woman had packed a bag full of other baby supplies for Maresa including formula, diapers, fresh clothes and linens, a gift funded by Cameron McNeill, she'd discovered. And while Maresa understood that the man could easily afford such generosity, she couldn't afford to accept any more after this day.

Today, she told herself, was an adjustment period. Tomorrow, she would have a plan.

Clutching the baby monitor the caregiver had provided, Maresa followed the scent of grilled meat toward the patio beside the pool. A woman in a white tuxedo shirt and crisp black pants bustled through the kitchen, her blond ponytail bobbing with her step. She nodded toward the French doors leading outside.

"Mr. McNeill said to tell you he has drinks ready right out here, unless you'd like to swim first, in which case there are suits in the bathhouse." She pointed to the left where a small cabana sat beside a gazebo.

"Thank you." Maresa's gaze flicked over the food the woman was assembling on the kitchen island—tiny appetizers with flaked fish balanced on thin slices of mango and endive, bright red crabmeat prepped for what looked like a shellfish soup and chopped vegetables for a conch salad. "It all looks delicious."

Her stomach growled with a reminder of how long it had been since her usual lunch hour had come and gone. Now, stepping outside onto the covered deck, Maresa spotted Cameron seated at a table beneath the gazebo, a bottled water in hand as he stared down at his laptop screen. Tropical foliage in colorful clay pots dotted the deck. The weathered teak furniture topped by thick cream-colored cushions was understated enough to let the view shine more than the decor. The call of birds and the distant roll of waves on the beach provided the kind of soundtrack other people piped in using a digital play-list in order to relax.

Seeing her, Cameron stood. The practice wasn't un-common in formal business meetings, and happened more often when she'd worked in Europe. But the ges-ture here, in this private place, felt more intimate since it was for her alone.

Or maybe she was simply too preoccupied with her boss.

"Did you find everything you needed?" he asked, tug-ging off the aviators he'd been wearing to set them on the graying teak table.

It was cool in the shade of the pergola threaded with bright pink bougainvillea, yet just being close to him made her skin warm. Her gaze climbed his tall height, stalling on his well-muscled shoulders before reaching his face. She took in the sculpted jaw and ice-blue eyes before shifting her focus to his lips. She hadn't kissed a man since her broken engagement.

A fact she hadn't thought about even once until right this moment.

"I'm fine," she blurted awkwardly, remembering she was there to work and not to catalog the finer masculine traits of the man whose family owned the company she worked for. "Ready to work."

Beneath the table, a dog yapped happily.

Maresa glanced down to see Poppy standing on a bright magenta dog bed. Beside the bed, a desk fan os-cillated back and forth, blowing through the dog's long white fur at regular intervals.

"Hello, Poppy." She leaned down to greet the fluffy pooch. "That's quite a setup you have there." She let the dog sniff her hand for a moment before she scratched behind the ears, not sure if Poppy would remember her.

"I had the dog walker pick up a few things to be sure she was comfortable. Plus, with a baby in the house, I thought she might be…you know. Jealous."

She looked up in time to see him shrug as if it was the most natural thought in the world to consider if his dog would be envious of an infant guest.

"That's adorable." She knew then that the Cameron Holmes character she'd met the day before had been all for show. Cameron McNeill was another man entirely. Although his jaw tightened at the "adorable" remark. She hurried to explain. "I mean, the dog bed and all of Poppy's matching accessories. Your mom found a lot of great things to coordinate the wardrobe."

Maresa rose to her feet, knowing she couldn't use the pup as a barrier all day.

"Actually, I borrowed Poppy from my brother's administrative assistant." He gestured to the seat beside him and turned the laptop to give her a better view. "I figured a fussy white show dog was a good way to test the patience and demeanor of the hotel staff. But I'll admit, she isn't nearly as uptight as I imagined." He patted the animal's head; the Maltese was rubbing affectionately against his ankles while he talked about her. "She's pretty great."

Coming around to his side of the table, Maresa took the seat he indicated. Right beside him. He'd changed into more casual clothes since she'd last seen him, his white cotton T-shirt only slightly dressed up by a pair of khakis and dark loafers. He wore some kind of brightly colored socks—aqua and purple—at odds with the rest of his outfit.

"The Carib is pet friendly, but I understand why you thought there might be pushback on demands like natural grass for the room." She glanced down at the laptop to see he'd left open a series of graphs with performance rankings for the Carib.

The downturn in the past two months was small, but noticeable.

"Ryegrass only," he reminded her. "I don't enjoy being tough on the staff, but I figured that playing undercover boss for a week or two would still be quicker and less painful for them than if I hire an independent agency to do a thorough review of operations."

"Of course." She gestured to the laptop controls. "May I look through this?"

At his nod, Maresa clicked on links and scrolled through the files related to the hotel's performance. Clearly, Cameron had been doing his homework, making margin notes throughout the document about the operations. Her name made frequent appearances, including a reference to an incident of misplaced money by a guest the week before.

"I remember this." Maresa's finger paused on the comment from a post-visit electronic survey issued to the guest. "An older couple reported that their travelers' checks had gone missing during a trip to the beach." She glanced up to see Cameron bent over the screen to read the notes, his face unexpectedly close to hers.

"The guy left the money in his jacket on the beach. It was gone when he returned." Cameron nodded, his jaw tense. "Definitely a vacation-ruiner."

She bristled. "But not the staff's fault. Our beach employees are tasked with making sure there are pool chairs and towels. We serve drinks and even bring food down to the cabanas. But we can't police everyone's possessions."

"On a private island where everyone should either be a guest or a staff member?" he asked with a hint of censure in his voice.

"That amounts to quite a few people," she pointed out, without hesitation. "And don't forget, many of our guests feel comfortable indulging in extra cocktails while vacationing."

"A few drinks won't make you think you had a thousand dollars in your pocket when you only had ten."

"Maybe not." She thrummed her fingernails on the teak table, remembering some of the antics she'd seen on the beach. Even before her work at the Carib, she'd seen plenty of visitors to Saint Thomas behave like springbreakers simply because they were far from home. Her father included. "However, a few drinks could make you think you put your money in your jacket when you actually had it in the pocket of the shorts you wore into the water, where you lost it while you tried to impress your trophy wife by doing backflips off a Jet Ski."

"And is that what happened in this case?" He glanced over at her, the woodsy scent of his aftershave teasing her senses.

"No." She shook her head, regretting the candid speech as much as the memory of her father's easy transition of affection from Maresa's mother to a wealthy female colleague. Today had rattled her. Her mind kept drifting back to Isla and what she would do tonight to keep her comfortable. "I'm sure it wasn't. I only meant to point out that the staff can't guard against some of the questionable decisions that guests make while vacationing."

Cam regarded her curiously. "I don't suppose your ex-fiancé has a trophy wife?"

"Jaden is still happily single from what I hear." She couldn't afford to share any more personal confidences with this man—her boss—who already knew far too much about her. To redirect their conversation, she tapped a few keys on his laptop. "These other incidents that guests wrote about on their comment forms—slow bar service, a disappointing gallery tour off-site—I assume you've looked into them?"

Both were news to her.

"The bar service, yes. The gallery tour, no. I don't suppose you know which tour they're referencing?"

"No one has asked me to arrange anything like this." She might not remember every hotel recommendation, but she certainly recalled specialty requests. "I can speak to some of the other staff members. Some guests like to ask the doormen or the waiters for their input on local sites."

"Good." He cleared a space in front of them on the table as a server came onto the patio with covered trays. "That's one of the drawbacks of maintaining a presence as a demanding guest—I can't very well quiz the staff for answers about things that happened last month."

Maresa watched as the server quickly set the table, filled their water glasses and left two platters behind along with a wine bottle in a clay pot to maintain the wine's temperature. The final thing the woman did was set out a fresh bowl of water for Poppy before she left them to their late lunch.

"I'm happy to help," Maresa told him honestly, relieved to know that the downturn in performance at the Carib was nothing tied to her work. Or her brother's. Their jobs were more important than ever with a baby to support.

"For that matter, I can't reveal the positive feedback we've received about the staff members either." Cameron lifted the wine bottle from the cooling container and inspected the label before pouring a pale white wine into her glass. "But I can tell you that Rafe received some glowing praise from a guest who referenced him by name."

"Really?" Pleased, Maresa helped herself to some of

the appetizers she'd seen inside, arranging a few extra pieces of mango beside the conch salad. "Did the guest say what he did?"

Cameron loaded his plate with ahi tuna and warm plantain chips with some kind of spicy-looking dipping sauce.

"Something about providing a 'happy escort' to the beach one day and lifting the guest's spirits by pointing out some native birds."

Rafe? Escorting a guest somewhere?

Maresa realized she'd been quiet a beat too long.

"Rafe loves birds," she replied truthfully, hating that she needed to mask her true thoughts with Cameron after he'd trusted her to give him honest feedback on the staff. "He does know a lot about the local plants and animals, too," she rushed to add. "That's one area of knowledge that his accident left untouched."

"Does it surprise you that he was escorting a guest to the beach?" Cameron studied her over his glass as he tasted the wine.

His blue eyes missed nothing.

Clearly, he would know Rafe's job description—something he'd have easy access to in his research of the performance reviews. There was no sense trying to deny it. Still, she hated feeling that she needed to defend her brother for doing a good job.

"A little," she admitted, her shoulders tense. Wary.

Before she could explain, however, a wail came through the baby monitor.

Cam hung back, unsure how to help while Maresa and the nurse caregiver discussed the baby's fretful state. Maresa held the baby close, shifting positions against her shoulder as the baby arched and squirmed.

Over half an hour after the infant's initial outburst, the

little girl still hadn't settled down. Her face was mottled and red, her hands flexing and straining, as if she fought unseen ghosts. Cam hated hearing the cries, but didn't have a clue what to offer. The woman he'd hired for the day was a nurse, after all. She would know if there was anything they needed to worry about, wouldn't she?

Still. He didn't blame Maresa for questioning her. Cameron had done some internet searches himself, one of the few things he knew to contribute.

A moment later, Maresa stepped out of the nursery and shut the door behind her, leaving Isla with Wendy. The cries continued. Poppy paced nervously outside the door.

"I should leave." Worry etched her features. She scraped back her sun-lightened curls behind one ear. "You've been so kind to help me manage my first day of caring for an infant, finding Wendy and the baby supplies, but I really can't impose any longer—"

"You are not anywhere close to an imposition." He didn't want her to leave. "I'm trying to help with Isla because I want to."

Maresa's hands fisted at her side, her whole body rigid. "She's my responsibility."

Her stubborn refusal reminded him of his oldest brother. Quinn never wanted anyone to help him either— a trait Cam respected, even when Quinn became too damn overbearing.

"You've know about her for less than twenty-four hours. Most families get nine months to prepare." He settled a hand on Maresa's shoulder, wanting to ease some of the weight she insisted on putting there.

"That doesn't make her any less my obligation." She folded her arms across her chest in a gesture that hovered between a defensive posture and an effort to hold herself together.

Another shriek from the nursery sent an answering spike of tension through Maresa; he could feel it under his fingertips. He'd have to be some kind of cretin not to respond to that. Still, he dropped his hand before he did something foolish like thread his fingers through her brown hair and soothe away the tension in her neck. Her back.

"Maybe not, but it gives you a damn good reason to accept some help until you get the legalities sorted out and come up with a game plan going forward." He extended his arms to gesture to the villa he'd taken for two weeks. "This place is going to be empty all evening once I head back to the hotel to put the Carib staffers through their paces. Stay put with Isla and the nurse. Have something to eat. Follow up with your lawyer. Poppy and I can sleep at the hotel tonight."

She shook her head. "I can't possibly accept such an offer. Even if you didn't own the company I work for, I couldn't allow you to do that."

"Ethics shouldn't rule out human kindness." Cameron wasn't going to rescind the offer because of some vague notion about what was right or proper. She needed help, damn it.

He drew her into a study down the hallway where indoor palm trees grew in a sunny corner under a series of skylights. Poppy trailed behind them, her collar jingling. Even here, the view of the water and the beach below was breathtaking. It made him want to cliff dive or wind surf. Or kiteboard.

He ground his teeth together on the last one. He hadn't been kiteboarding since the accident that ensured he'd never have children of his own. As if the universe had conspired to make sure he didn't repeat his father's mistakes.

"Is that what this is?" She stared up at him with questioning eyes. Worried. "Kindness? Because to be quite honest, this day has felt like a bit more than that, starting down at the beach this morning."

Starting yesterday for him, actually.

So he couldn't pretend not to know what she meant.

"There may be an underlying dynamic at work, yes. But that doesn't mean I can't offer to do something kind for you on an impossibly hard day." He had that ability, damn it. He wasn't totally self-absorbed. "And it's not just for you. It's for your brother, who might need more time to deal with this. And for Isla, who is clearly unhappy. Why not make their day easier, too?"

Maresa was quiet a long moment.

"What underlying dynamic?" she asked finally.

"It's not obvious?" He turned on his heel, needing a minute to weigh how much he wanted to spell things out. Go on the record. But he did, damn it. He liked this woman. He liked her fearless strength for her family, taking on their problems with more fierceness than she exercised for herself. Who took care of her? "I'm attracted to you."

He wasn't sure what kind of reaction he expected. But if he had to guess, he wouldn't have anticipated an argument.

"No." Her expression didn't change, the unflappable concierge facade in full play. "That's not possible."

There was a flash of fire in her tawny eyes, though. He'd bank on that.

"For all of my shortcomings, I'm pretty damn sure I know what attraction feels like."

"I didn't mean that. It's just—" She closed her eyes for a moment, as if she needed that time in the dark to collect her thoughts. When she opened them again, she took a deep breath. "I don't think I have the mental and emotional wherewithal to figure out what that means right now and what the appropriate response should be." She tipped two fingers to the bridge of her nose and pressed. "I can't afford to make a decision I'll regret. This job is...everything to me. And now I need it more than ever if I'm going to take proper care of Isla and my brother."

"I understand." Now that he'd admitted the attraction, he realized how strong it was, and that rattled him more than a little. He was here for business, not pleasure. "And I'm not acting on those feelings because I don't want to add to the list of things you need to worry about."

"Okay." She eyed him warily. "Thank you."

"So here's what I propose. I'm going to need your help on this project. It's important to me." He couldn't afford trouble at the Carib with so much riding on the Caribbean expansion program. The McNeills had their hands full with their grandfather's failing health and three more heirs on the horizon to vie for the family legacy. "Take a couple of days off from the hotel. Stay here with Isla and get acquainted with her while you prepare your family and plan your next steps. I'll stay at the hotel with Poppy."

"Cam—"

"No arguments." He really needed to leave her be so she could settle in and connect with the baby. He understood the crying and the newness of the situation would upset anyone, especially a woman accustomed to running things smoothly. "You can review those files I showed you earlier in more detail. I'd like your assessment of a variety of hotel personnel."

Finally, she nodded. It felt like a major victory. And no matter what he'd said about ignoring the attraction, he couldn't help but imagine what it would be like to have her agree to other things he wanted from her. Having dinner with him, for instance. Letting him taste her full lips. Feeling her soft curves beneath his palms.

"Isla and I can't thank you enough." She backed away from him and reached for the door. "I should really go check on her."

"Don't wear yourself out," he warned. "Share the duties with the nurse."

"I will." She smiled, her hand pausing on the door-knob, some of the tension sliding off her shoulders.

"And that Jeep we used to get here actually goes with the property. I'll leave the keys on the kitchen counter and have a plate sent up from the kitchen for you." He wasn't going out of his way, he told himself. It was easy enough to do that for her.

Or was he deluding himself? He wanted Maresa— pure and simple. But he knew it was more than that. Something about her drew him. Made him want to help her. He could do this much, at least, with a clear con-science. It benefitted McNeill Resorts to have her re-view those reports. He was simply giving her the time and space to do the job.

"But how will you get back to the hotel?"

"Poppy is ready for a walk." He could use a long trek to cool off. Remind himself why he had no business act-ing on what he was feeling for Maresa. "We'll take the scenic route along the beach." He held up his phone. "I'll leave my number with the keys downstairs. Call if you need anything."

"Okay." She nodded, then tipped her head to one side, her whole body going still. "Oh wow. Do you hear that?"

"What?" He listened.

"She stopped crying." Maresa looked relieved. Happy. So it was a total surprise that she burst into tears.

Five

If Maresa hadn't needed her job so badly, she would have seriously considered resigning.

Never in her life had she done anything so embarrassing as losing control in front of an employer. But the day had been too much, from start to finish. After the intense stress of listening to Isla cry for forty minutes, she'd been so relieved to hear silence reign in the nursery. The sudden shift of strong emotions had tipped something inside her.

Now, much to her extreme mortification, Cameron McNeill's arms were around her as he drew her onto a cushioned gray settee close to the door. Even more embarrassing? How much she wanted to sink into those arms and wail her heart out on his strong chest. She cried harder.

"It's okay," he assured her, his voice beside her ear and his woodsy aftershave stirring a hunger for closeness she could not afford.

"No, it's really not." She shook her head against his shoulder, telling herself to get it together.

"As your boss, I order you to stop arguing with me."

She couldn't stop a watery laugh. "I don't know what's the matter with me."

"Anyone would be overwhelmed right now." His arms tightened, drawing her closer in a way that was undeniably more comfortable. "Don't fight so damn hard. Let it out."

And for a moment, she did just that. She didn't let herself think about how deeply she'd screwed up by sobbing in his arms. She just let the emotions run through her, the whole great big unwieldy mess that her life had become. She hadn't cried like this when the doctor told her Rafe might not live. Day after day, she'd sat in that hospital and willed him to hang on and fight. Then, by the time he finally opened his eyes again, she couldn't afford to break down. She needed to be strong for him. To show him that she was fighting, too.

She'd helped him relearn to walk. Had that really been just six months ago? He'd come so far, so fast. But she knew there were limits to what he could do.

Limits to how much he could do because she willed it. She knew, in her heart, he would not be able to handle a crying baby even if she could make him understand that Isla was his. It wouldn't be right to thrust this baby into his life right now. Or fair.

She didn't need the counselor to tell her that, even though the woman had finally returned her call and left a message to come by the office in the morning. Maresa knew that the woman was trying to find a way to tell her the hard truth—this baby could upset him so much he could have a setback.

And she cried for that. For him. Because there had

been a time in Rafe's life when the birth of his daughter would have been a cause for celebration. It broke her
heart that his life had to be so different now.

With one last shuddering sigh, she felt the storm inside
her pass. As it eased away, leaving her drained but more
at peace, Maresa became aware of the man holding her.
Aware of the hard plane of his chest where her forehead
rested. Of the warm skin beneath the soft cotton T-shirt
that she'd soaked with her tears. Amidst all the other em-
barrassments of the day she was at least grateful that her
mascara had been waterproof. It would have been one
indignity too many to leave her makeup on his clothes.

His arm was around her shoulders, his hand on her
upper arm where he rubbed gentle circles that had
soothed her a moment before. Now? That touch teased a
growing awareness that spread over her skin to make her
senses sing. With more than a little regret, she levered
herself up, straightening.

"Cameron." Her voice raspy from the crying, his name
sounded far too intimate when she said it that way.

Then again, maybe it seemed more intimate since she
was suddenly nose-to-nose with him, his arm still holding
her close. She forgot to think. Forgot to breathe. She was
pretty sure her heart paused, too, as she stared up at him.

A sexy, incredibly appealing man.

Without her permission, her fingers moved to his face.
She traced the line of his lightly shadowed jaw, surprised
at the rough bristle against her fingertips. His blue eyes
hypnotized her. There was simply no other explanation
for what was happening to her right now. Her brain told
her to extricate herself. Walk away.

Her hands had other ideas. She twined them around
his neck, her heart full of a tenderness she shouldn't

feel. But he'd been so good to her. So thoughtful. And she wanted to kiss him more than she wanted anything.

"Maresa." Her name on his lips was a warning. A chance to change her mind.

She understood that she was pushing a boundary. Recognized that he'd just drawn a line in the sand.

"I didn't mind giving up my dream job in Paris to care for Rafe and help my mother recover," she confided, giving him absolutely no context for her comment and hoping he understood what she was saying. "And I will gladly give eighteen years to raise my niece as my own daughter." She'd known it without question the moment Jaden handed her Isla. "But I'm not sure I can sacrifice the chance to have this kiss."

She'd crossed the boundary. Straight into "certifiable" territory. She must have cried out all her good sense.

His blue eyes simmered with more heat than a Saint Thomas summer. He cupped her chin, cradling her face like she was something precious.

"If I thought you wouldn't regret it tomorrow, I'd give you all the kisses you could handle." The stroke of his thumb along her cheek didn't begin to soothe the rejection.

Her eyes burned again, reminding her just how jumbled her emotions were right now. Knowing he had a point did nothing to salvage her pride.

"You told me you were attracted to me." She unwound her hands from his neck.

"Too much," he admitted. "That's why I'm trying to be smart about this. I'm willing to wait to be with you until a time when you won't have any regrets about it."

"You say that like it's a foregone conclusion." She straightened, her cheeks heating.

"Or maybe it's using the power of positive thinking." His lips kicked up in a half smile, but she needed air. Space.

"You should go." She wanted time to clear her head.

Tipping her head toward him, he kissed her forehead with a gentle tenderness that made her ache for all she couldn't have.

"I'll see you in the morning," he told her, shoving to his feet.

"I thought I was taking time off?" She tucked her disheveled hair behind one ear, eager to call her mother and figure out what to do about Isla.

"From the hotel. Not from me." He shoved his hands in his pockets, and something about the gesture made her think he'd done it to keep from touching her.

She knew because she felt the same need to touch him.

"When will I see you?"

"Text me when you and Isla are ready in the morning and I'll come get you. I'm traveling to Martinique tomorrow and I'd like you with me."

She arched an eyebrow. "You need a tour guide with an infant in tow?"

"We could talk through some of the data in those reports a bit more. You could help give me a bigger picture of what's going on here." He opened the door into the quiet hallway of the expansive vacation villa. "Besides, I want to be close by if you decide you want to share kisses you won't regret down the road."

He strode away, whistling softly for Poppy as he headed toward the main staircase. He left Maresa alone in the extravagant house with a baby, a nurse and all kinds of confused feelings for him. One thing was certain, though.

A man like Cameron McNeill might tempt her sorely. But he was a fantasy. A temporary escape from the reality of a life full of obligations she would never walk away from. So until her heart understood how thoroughly off-limits he was, Maresa needed to put all thoughts of kisses out of her head.

An hour later, Maresa had her mother in the Jeep with her as she pulled up to the gated vacation villa. She'd calmly explained the Isla situation on a phone call on the way over to her house, arranging for their retired neighbor to visit with Rafe for a couple of hours while Maresa brought her mom to meet her grandchild.

After hearing back from Rafe's counselor that a mention of his daughter could trigger too much frustration and a possible memory block, Maresa had simply told her brother she wanted to bring their mother to meet a girlfriend's new baby.

She'd kept the story simple and straightforward, and Rafe didn't mind the visit time with Mr. Leopold, who was happy to play one of Rafe's video games with him and keep an eye on him. The paperwork requesting temporary legal custody of the baby would be filed in the morning by her attorney, so she'd taken care of that, too.

Now, driving through the gates, Maresa enjoyed her mother's startled gasp at the breathtaking view of the Caribbean.

"I had the same reaction earlier," she admitted, halting the Jeep in the space beside the nurse's sedan. "But this isn't half as beautiful as Isla."

"I cannot wait to meet her." Analise Delphine opened the car door slowly, the neuropathy in her hands one of many nerve conditions caused by her MS. "But I'm still so angry at Trina for not telling us sooner. Can you imagine what happiness it would have given us in those dark hours with your brother if we had only known about his daughter?"

Maresa hurried around the car to help her mother out since it did no good to tell her to wait. Analise had struggled more with her disease ever since the car crash that injured Rafe. Maresa worried about her since her mother seemed to blame herself—and her MS—for the injury to her beloved son, and some days it appeared as if she wanted to suffer because of her guilt. For months, Maresa had encouraged her mother to get into some more family counseling, but Analise would only go to sessions that were free through a local clinic, not wanting to "be a burden."

Maresa had tread lightly around the topic until now, but if they were going to be responsible for this baby, she needed her mother to be strong emotionally even if her physical health was declining.

"Trina is young," Maresa reminded her as she helped her up the white stone walkway to the main entrance of the villa. "She must have been scared and confused between finding out she was pregnant and then learning Rafe wasn't going to make a full recovery."

Analise breathed heavily as she leaned on Maresa's arm. Analise had always been the most beautiful girl on the block, according to their neighbor Mr. Leopold. She'd worked as a dancer in clubs and in street performances for tourists, earning a good living for years before the MS hit her hard. Her limber dancer's body had thickened with her inability to move freely, but her careful makeup and her eye for clothing meant she always looked stage-ready.

"She is old enough to make better choices." Her mother stopped abruptly, squinting into the sunlight as she peered up at the vacation home. "Speaking of which, Maresa, I hope you are making wise choices by staying here. You said your boss is allowing you to do this?"

"Yes, Mom." She tugged gently at her mother's arm, drawing her up the wide stone steps. "He was there when Jaden handed me Isla, so he knew I had a lot to contend with today."

She wasn't sure about the rest of his motives. She was still separating Cameron McNeill from surly Mr. Holmes, trying to understand him. He'd walked out on her today when she would have gladly lost herself in the attraction. Some of her wounded pride had been comforted by his assurance that he wanted her.

So where did that leave them for tomorrow when he expected her to accompany him to a neighboring island?

"Most men don't share their expensive villas without expectations, Maresa. Be smarter than that," her mother chastised her while Maresa unlocked the front door with the key Cameron had left behind. "You need to come home."

Before she could argue, Wendy appeared in the foyer, a pink bundle in her arms. Her mother oohed and aahed, mesmerized by her new grandchild as she happily cataloged all the sleeping baby's features. Maresa paid scant attention, however, as Analise declared the hairline was Rafe's and the mouth inherited was from Analise herself.

Maresa still smarted from her mother's insistence that she wasn't "being smart" to stay in the villa with Isla tonight. Perhaps it stung all the more because that had been Maresa's first instinct, as well. But damn it, Cameron had a point about the practicality of it. The Carib did indeed comp rooms to special guests who provided services. Why couldn't she enjoy the privilege while she helped Cameron McNeill investigate the operations of his luxury hotel?

Putting aside her frustration, she tried to enjoy her mother's pleasure in the baby even as Maresa worried about the future. It was easy for her mom to tell her that she should simply bring Isla home, but it would be Maresa who had to make arrangements for caregiving and Maresa who would wake up every few hours to look after the child. All of their lives were going to change dramatically under the roof of her mother's tiny house.

Maybe she needed to look for a larger home for all of them. She'd thought she couldn't afford it before, but now she wondered how she could afford *not* to buy something bigger. She would speak to her mother about it, but first, it occurred to her she could speak to Cameron. He was a businessman. His brother—she'd once read online—was a hedge fund manager. Surely a McNeill could give sound financial advice.

Besides, talking about the Caribbean housing market would be a welcome distraction in case the conversation ever turned personal tomorrow. If ever she was tempted to kiss him again, she'd just think about interest rates. That ought to cool her jets in a hurry.

"Look, Maresa!" Her mother turned the baby on her lap to show her Isla's face as they sat on the loveseat of a sprawling white family room decorated with dark leather furnishings and heavy Mexican wood. The little girl's eyes were open now, blinking owlishly. "She has your father's eyes! We need to call him and tell him. He won't believe it."

"Mom. No." She reached for the baby while Analise dug in her boho bag sewn out of brightly colored fabric scraps and pulled out a cell phone. "Dad never likes hearing from us."

She'd been devastated by her father's furious reaction to her phone call the night of Rafe's accident.

I've moved on, Maresa. Help your mother get that through her head.

"Nonsense." Analise grinned as she pressed the screen. "He'll want to hear this. Isla is his first grandchild, too, you know."

In Maresa's arms, the infant kicked and squirmed, her back arching as if she were preparing for a big cry. Maresa resisted the urge to call to Wendy, needing the experience of soothing the little girl. So she patted her back and spoke comforting words, shooting to her feet to walk around the room while her mother left a message on her father's voice mail. No surprise he hadn't picked up the call.

"I bet he'll book a flight down here as soon as he can," Analise assured her. "I should be getting home so I can make the house ready for company. And a baby, too!"

She levered slowly out of her chair to her feet, her new energy and excitement making her wince less even though the hurt had to be just the same as it was an hour ago.

"I don't think Dad will come down here," Maresa warned her quietly, not wanting her mom's hopes raised to impossible levels.

Jack Janson hadn't returned once since moving overseas. He hadn't even visited Maresa in Paris; she'd briefly hoped that since he lived in the UK, he might make the effort to see her. But no.

"Could you let me be excited about just this one thing? We have enough to worry us, Maresa. Let's look for things to be hopeful about." She put her hand on Maresa's shoulders, a touch that didn't comfort her in the least.

If anything, Maresa remembered why she needed to be all the more careful with Cameron McNeill. Like her father, he was only here on business. Like her father, he might think it was fun to indulge himself with a local woman while he was far from his home and his real life.

But once he left Saint Thomas and solved the problems at the Carib Grand, Maresa knew all too well that he wasn't ever coming back.

Cameron had new respect for the running abilities of Maltese show dogs.

He sprinted through the undergrowth on the beach the next morning, about an hour after sunrise, trying to keep up with the little pooch.

"Poppy!" he called to her, cursing himself for giving her a moment off the leash. He'd scoped the beach and knew they were alone on the Carib Grand's private stretch of shore, so he'd figured it was okay.

He could keep up with the little dog on her short legs after all. But Poppy was small and shifty, darting and zigzagging through the brush where Cam couldn't fit. The groomer was going to think he'd gotten the pup's fur tangled on purpose, but damn it, he was just trying to let her have some fun. She seemed so happy chasing those terns.

If only it was as easy to tell what would make Maresa Delphine happy. He'd spent most of the day with her and still wasn't sure how to make her smile again. The concierge had the weight of the world on her straight shoulders.

Catching sight of muddy white fur, Cameron swooped low to scoop up the dog in midstride.

"Gotcha." He held on to the wriggling, overexcited bundle of wet canine while she tried her best to lick his face.

He'd have to shower again before his day in Martinique with Maresa since he was now covered with beach sand and dog fur, but it was tough to stay perturbed with the overjoyed animal. Chiding her gently while he attached the leash, Cam turned to go back up the path to the hotel.

Only to spot Rafe Delphine walking toward the beach beside a well-dressed, much older woman.

Surprised that Rafe had come in to work with Maresa taking the day off, Cameron watched the pair from a hidden vantage point in the bushes.

"Do you know this painter I'm meeting, young man?" the woman asked, her accent sounding Nordic, maybe. Or Finnish.

The woman was probably in her late sixties or early seventies. She had a sleek blond bob and expensive-looking bag. Even the beach sandals she wore had the emblem of an exclusive designer Cam recognized because a long-ago girlfriend had dragged him to a private runway show.

"Jaden paints." Rafe nodded his acknowledgement of the question but his eye was on the ground where a bird flapped its damp wings. "Look. A tern."

Poppy wriggled excitedly. The movement attracted the older woman's attention, giving up Cam's hiding place She smiled at him.

"What a precious little princess!" she exclaimed, eyes on Poppy. "She looks like she's been having fun today."

Rafe's tawny eyes—so like his sister's—turned his way. He gave Cam a nod of recognition, or maybe it was just politeness. Effectively called out of his spot in the woods, Cameron stepped into the sunlight and let the woman meet Poppy, who was—as always—appropriately gracious for the attention.

After a brief exchange with the dog, Cameron continued toward the hotel. He'd known that Jaden Torries was probably trolling for work at the Carib, so it shouldn't be a huge surprise that one of the hotel guests was meeting him at the beach. But why was Rafe bringing her to meet him?

Given how much Maresa disliked her ex-fiancé, it seemed unlikely she would be the one facilitating Jaden doing any kind of work with hotel patrons. Especially since she wasn't even working today. Then again, what if she had found a way to make a little extra income by helping Jaden find patrons? Would she set aside her distaste for him if it made things easier for her?

Deep in thought, Cam arrived at the pool deck. He didn't want to think his attraction to Maresa would influence his handling of the situation, but his first instinct was to speak to her directly. He would ask her about it when he picked her up at the villa, he decided.

Except then he spotted her circulating among the guests by the pool. She'd been here all along?

Suspicion mounted. Grinding his teeth, he charged toward her, more than ready for some answers.

Six

Morning sun beating down on her head, Maresa noticed Cameron McNeill heading her way and she braced herself for the resurrection of Mr. Holmes. She knew he needed to be undercover to learn more about the hotel operations, but did he have to be quite so convincing in his "difficult guest" role? The hard set of his jaw and brooding glare were seriously intimidating even knowing how kind he could be.

She straightened from a conversation with one of her seasonal guests from Quebec who rented a suite for half the year. Pasting on a professionally polite smile to greet Cameron, she told herself she should be grateful to see this side of him so she wouldn't be tempted to throw herself at him again.

Even if his bare chest and low-slung board shorts drew every female eye.

"Good morning, Mr. Holmes." She reached to smooth

her jacket sleeves, only to remember she'd worn a sundress today for the trip into Martinique. *Oh, my.* Her skin had goose bumps of awareness just from standing this close to him.

"May I speak to you privately?" He handed off Poppy to the dog groomer who scurried over from where he'd been waiting by the tiki bar.

Cameron certainly couldn't have any complaints about the service he was receiving, could he? People seemed to hurry to offer him assistance.

"Of course." She excused herself from the other guests, following him toward the door marked Employees Only.

He didn't slow his step until they were in the same conference room where they'd spoken yesterday. The cool blast of air almost matched the ice chips in his blue eyes. He shoved the door shut behind them before he turned to face her.

"I thought you were taking the day off from the hotel." His jaw flexed and he crossed his arms over his bare chest, the board shorts riding low on his hips.

She tried not to stare, distracting herself by focusing on the hint of confrontation in his tone.

"I am." She gestured to her informal clothing. "I only stopped by this morning to see my brother and make sure he felt comfortable about his workday."

"And is he comfortable escorting guests to the beach?" Cameron's arctic glare might have made another woman shiver. Maresa straightened her spine.

"I never give him jobs like that. Why do you ask?" Defensiveness for her brother roared through her.

"Because I just saw him walking one of our overseas guests to the shore to meet Jaden Torries."

Surprised, she quickly guessed he must be mistaken.

He had to be. Still a hint of tension tickled her gut. "Rafe doesn't even arrive until the next ferry." She checked her watch just to be sure the day hadn't slipped away from her. "He should be walking in the employee locker rooms any minute to punch his time card."

"He's already here." Cameron pulled out one of the high-backed leather chairs for her, all sorts of muscles flexing as he moved, distracting her when she needed to be focused. "I saw him myself at the beach with one of the hotel guests just a few minutes ago."

"I don't understand." Ignoring the seat, she paced away from all that tempting male muscle to peer out the windows overlooking the croquet lawn near the pool, hoping to get a view of the path to the beach. How could she relax, wondering if her brother might be doing jobs around the Carib without her knowing? She was supposed to watch over him during his first few months of employment. She'd promised the hotel director as much. "I got here early so I wouldn't miss him when he came to work. I want everything to go smoothly for him if I'm not here to supervise him myself."

Cameron joined her at the window, his body warm beside hers as he peered out onto the mostly empty side lawns. A butterfly garden near the window attracted a handful of brightly colored insects. His shoulder brushed hers, setting off butterflies inside, too. She hated feeling this way—torn between the physical attraction and the mental frustration.

"Did you know Jaden was soliciting business from hotel guests?" Cameron's question was quiet. Dispassionate.

And it offended her mightily. How dare he question her integrity? Her work record was impeccable and he should know as much if he was even halfway doing *his* job.

Anger burned through her as she whirled to face him, her skirt brushing his leg he stood so close to her. She took a step back.

"Absolutely not. Until yesterday, I hadn't seen Jaden since I left for Paris two years ago." She frowned, not understanding why Cameron would think she'd do such a thing. "And while I don't wish him ill, my relationship with him is absolutely over. I certainly don't have any desire to risk my job to help a man I dislike profit off our guests."

"I see." Cameron nodded slowly, as if weighing whether or not to believe her.

Worry balled in her stomach and she reined in her anger. She couldn't afford to be offended. She needed him to believe her.

"Why would you think I'd do such a thing?" She didn't want to be here. She wanted to find her brother and ask him what was going on.

Did Rafe even understand what he was doing by helping Jaden meet potential clients for his artwork? Was Jaden asking him for that kind of help?

"That type of business is probably lucrative for him—"

Understanding dawned. Indignation flared, hot and fast. "And you thought I would be a part of some sordid scheme with my ex-fiancé for the sake of extra cash? Even twisting my brother's arm into setting up meetings when I do everything in my power to protect him?"

If it had been anyone else, she would have stormed out of the meeting room. But she needed this job too much and, at the end of the day, Cameron McNeill was still an owner of the Carib.

He held all the cards.

"I don't know what to think. That's why I wanted to speak to you privately." He picked up a gray T-shirt from the back of a chair in the conference room and pulled it over his head.

She watched in spite of herself, realizing he must have been doing work in the conference room earlier that morning since a laptop and phone sat on the table.

"I won't have any answers until I speak to my brother." She was worried about him. For him. For the baby. Oh God, when had life gotten so complicated?

What had her brother gotten into?

"You realize this isn't the first time he's done it." Cameron's voice softened as he headed toward her again. "That customer review that I shared with you yesterday was from someone who said he provided a 'happy escort' to the beach." Cameron's blue eyes probed hers, searching for answers she didn't have.

As much as she longed to share her fears with him, she couldn't do that. Not when he was in charge of her fate at the hotel, and Rafe's, too.

"I remember." She itched to leave, needing to see Rafe for herself. "And now that you've put that comment in context, I'm happy to speak to my brother and clear this up."

She turned toward the door, desperate to put the complicated knot of feelings her boss inspired behind her.

"Wait." Cameron reached for her hand and held it, his touch warm and firm. "I realize you want to protect him, Maresa, but we need to find out what's going on."

"And we will," she insisted, wishing he didn't make her heart beat faster. "Just as soon as I speak to him."

Cameron studied her for a long moment with searching eyes, then quietly asked, "What if he doesn't have a clear answer?"

Some of the urgency eased from her. She couldn't deny that was a possibility.

"I can only do my best to figure out what's going on." She couldn't imagine who else would be giving him extra chores to do around the hotel. Rafe had never particularly liked Jaden. Then again, her brother was a different man since the accident.

"I know that. And what if we learn more by observing him for a few days? Maybe it would be better to simply keep a closer eye on him now that we know he's carrying out duties for the hotel—or someone else—that you haven't authorized." His tone wasn't accusing. "Maybe you shouldn't upset him unnecessarily."

She wanted to tell him she already spent hours supervising her brother. More than others on her staff. But she bit her lip, refusing to reveal a piece of information that could get Rafe terminated from his position.

"I don't want him getting hurt," she argued, worried about letting her brother's behavior continue unchecked. "And I don't know who he's speaking to that would advise him to take risks like this with his job."

The day had started out so promising, with Isla sleeping for five hours straight and waking up with a drooly baby smile, only to take this radical nosedive. Anxiety spiked. Rafe was going to lose this job, damn it. She would never be able to afford a caregiver for Isla and a companion to supervise Rafe, too. Especially not once they lost Rafe's income. Heaven only knew how much he would recover from the brain injury. What kind of future he would have? How much he could provide for himself, much less a child? All the fears of the unknown jumped up inside her.

Cameron hissed a low, frustrated breath between his teeth. "What if we compromise? You confront him now, but if you don't get a direct answer or if you sense there's more to his answer than what he shares, you back off.

Then, we can keep a closer eye on him for the next week and see who is setting up these meetings."

She didn't like the idea of waiting. She knew there was a good chance Rafe wouldn't give her a direct answer. But what choice did she really have? She wouldn't be able to push him anyhow, since his health and potential recovery were more important than getting answers to any mystery going on at the Carib.

"Fine." She turned to the door, eager to see her brother, but she paused when Cameron followed her. "I'd prefer to speak to him alone."

He followed her so closely that she needed to tilt her head to peer up at him.

"Of course." He stood near enough that she could see the shades of blue in his eyes, as varied as the Caribbean. "I'm going to change for our trip. I'll have a car meet you out front in fifteen minutes."

She wondered if it was wise to risk being seen leaving the hotel with surly Mr. Holmes. But then, that wasn't her problem so much as his. She had enough to worry about waiting for the DNA tests to come back so she could finally tell Rafe about Isla. Her lawyer and his psychologist had advised her and her mother to wait until then.

Hurrying away from all that distracting masculine appeal, Maresa rushed into the employee lounge to look for her brother. She'd already called in a favor from Big Bill, the head doorman, to help keep an eye on Rafe for the next few days. Bill was a friend of her mother's from their old neighborhood and he'd been kind enough to agree, but Maresa knew the man could only do so much.

Inside the lounge, the scent of morning coffee mingled with someone's too-strong perfume. A few people from the maintenance staff gossiped around the kitchen table where a box of pastries sat open. Moving past the kitchen,

Maresa peered into the locker area between the men's and women's private lounges. Rafe sat in the middle row of lockers, carefully braiding the stems of yellow buttercups into a chain. Flowers spilled over the polished bench as he straddled it, his focus completely absorbed in the task.

Any frustration she felt with him melted away. How could Cameron think for a moment that her brother would knowingly do anything unethical at work? It was only because Cameron didn't know Rafe. If he did, he'd never think something like that for a moment.

"Hey, Rafe." She took a seat on the bench nearby, wishing with all her heart he could be in a work program designed for people with his kinds of abilities. He had so much to offer with his love of nature and talent with green and growing things. Even now, his affinity for plants was evident, the same as before the accident when he'd had his own landscaping business. "What are you making?"

He glanced up at her, his eyes so like the ones she saw in the mirror every day.

"Maresa." He smiled briefly before returning his attention to the flowers. "I'm making you a bracelet."

"Me?" She had worried he was heaping more gifts on Nancy. And while she liked the server, she didn't want Rafe to have any kind of romantic hopes about the woman. Hearing the flowers were for her was a relief.

"I felt bad I left work." He lifted the flower chain and laid it on her wrist, his shirt cuffs brushing her skin as he carefully knotted the stems together. "I'm sorry."

Her heart knotted up like the flowers.

"Thank you. I love it." She kissed him on the cheek, smiling at the way his simple offering looked beside the silver star bracelet he'd given her two years ago before she left for Paris.

He was as thoughtful as ever, and his way of showing it hadn't changed all that much.

"Rafe?" She drew a deep breath, hating to ruin a happy moment with questions about Jaden. But this was important. The sooner she helped Cameron McNeill figure out what was going on at the Carib Grand, the sooner their jobs would be secure and they could focus on a new life with Isla—if Isla was in fact his child. And even though their lives would be less complicated without the child, Maresa couldn't deny that the thought of Isla leaving made her stomach clench. "Why did you go to the beach this morning?"

She kept the question simple. Direct.

"Mr. Ricci asked." Rafe rose to his feet, dusting flower petals off his faded olive cargoes. "Time to go to work. Mom said I don't work with you today."

She blinked at the fast change of topic. "Mr. Ricci asked you to bring a guest to the beach?"

"It's eight thirty." Rafe pointed to his watch. "Mom said I don't work with you today."

Damn it. Damn it. She didn't want to throw his whole workday off for the sake of a conversation that might lead nowhere. Maybe Cameron was right and they were better off keeping an eye on the situation.

"Right. I have to work off-site today. You'll be helping Glenna at the concierge stand, but Big Bill is on duty today. If you need help with anything, ask Bill, okay?"

"Ask Big Bill." Rafe gave her a thumbs-up before he stalked out of the locker room and into the hotel to start work.

Watching him leave, Maresa's fingers went to the bracelet he'd made her. He was thoughtful and kind. Surely he would have so much to give Isla. She needed to speak to his counselor in more detail so they could brainstorm ideas for the right way to introduce them. It seemed wrong to deprive the little girl of a father when her mother had already given up on her.

For now, however, she needed to tell Cameron that Rafe was escorting guests to the beach because the hotel director told him to. Would Cameron believe her? Or would he demand to speak to her brother himself?

Cameron's seductive promise floated back to her. *If I thought you wouldn't regret it tomorrow, I'd give you all the kisses you could handle.* She'd replayed those words again and again since he'd said them.

She walked a tightrope with her compelling boss— needing him to allow Rafe to stay in his job, but needing her own secured even more. Which meant she had to help him in his investigation.

Most of all, to keep those objectives perfectly clear, she had to ignore her growing attraction to him. His kindness with Isla might have slid past her defenses, but in order to protect the baby's future, Maresa would have to set aside her desire to find out what "all the kisses she could handle" would feel like.

The flight to Martinique was fast and efficient. They took off from the private dock near the Carib Grand's beach and touched down in the Atlantic near Le Francois on the east coast of Martinique. The pilot landed the new seaplane smoothly, barely jostling Baby Isla's carrier where she sat beside Maresa in the seats facing Cameron.

Cameron tried to focus on the baby to keep his mind off the exotically gorgeous woman across from him. The task had been damn near impossible for the hour of flight time between islands. Maresa's bright sundress was so different from the linen suits he'd seen her in for work. He liked the full skirt and vibrant poppy print, and he admired that she wore the simple floral bracelet around one wrist. With her hair loose and sun-tipped around her face, she looked impossibly beautiful. Her movements with Isla were easier today and her fascination with the little girl was obvious every time she glanced Isla's way.

Before she unbuckled the baby's carrier, she pressed a kiss to the infant's smooth forehead. A new pink dress with a yellow bunny on the front had been a gift from Maresa's mother, apparently. They'd spoken about that much on that flight. Maresa had given him an update on the custody paperwork with the lawyer, the paternity test she'd ordered using Rafe's hair and a cheek swab of Isla's, and she'd told him about her mother's reaction to her granddaughter. They'd only discussed Rafe briefly, agreeing not to confront him any further about bringing guests to meet Jaden Torries. They would watch Rafe more carefully when they returned to Saint Thomas. Until then, Bill the doorman knew to keep a close eye on him.

Cameron hadn't pushed her to discuss her theory about what might be going on, knowing that she was already worried about her brother's activities at the hotel. But at some point today, they would have to discuss where to go next with Rafe, and Jaden, too. For now, Cameron simply wanted to put her at ease for a few hours while he gathered some information about this secret branch of his family. The Martinique McNeills had a home in Le Francois, an isolated compound that was the equivalent of Grandfather Malcolm's home in Manhattan—a centrally located hub with each of the brothers' names on the deed. The family had other property holdings, but their mother had lived here before her death and the next generation all spent time there.

Cameron had done his homework and was ready to

check out this group today. Later, after Maresa had time to relax and catch her breath from the events of the last few days, he would talk to her about a plan for the future. For her and for Isla, too. The little girl in the pink dress tugged at his heart.

"So you have family here?" Maresa passed the baby carrier to him while the pilot opened the plane door.

Fresh air blew in, toying lightly with Maresa's hair.

"In theory. Yes." He wasn't happy about the existence of the other McNeills. "That is—they don't know we're related yet. My father kept his other sons and mistress a secret. When his lover tired of being hidden, she sold the house he'd bought her and left without a forwarding address. He didn't fight her legally because of the scandal that would create." As he said it aloud, however, he realized that didn't sound like his father. "Actually, he was probably just too disinterested to try and find them. He never paid us much attention either."

Liam McNeill had been a sorry excuse for a father. Cameron refused to follow in those footsteps.

Cam lifted the baby carrier above the seats, following Maresa to the exit. They'd parked at a private dock for the Cap Est Lagoon, a resort hotel in Le Francois close to the McNeill estate.

"But at least he's still a part of your life, isn't he?" Maresa held her full skirt with one hand as she descended the steps of the plane. A gusty breeze wreaked havoc with the hem.

The view of her legs was a welcome distraction during a conversation about his dad.

"He is part of the business, so I see him at company meetings. But it's not like he shows up for holidays to hang out. He's never been that kind of father." Even Cameron's grandfather hadn't quite known what to do to create a sense of family. Sure, he'd taken in Quinn, Ian and Cameron often enough as teens. But they were more apt to travel with him on business, learning the ropes from the head of the company, than have fun.

Luckily, Cam had had his brothers.

And, later, his own reckless sense of fun.

Maresa held her hair with one hand as they walked down the dock together, the baby between them in her seat. Behind them, the hotel staff unloaded their bags from the seaplane. Not that they'd travelled with much, but Cam had taken a suite here so Maresa would have a place to retreat with Isla. The Cap Est spread out on the shore ahead of them, the red-roofed buildings ringing the turquoise lagoon. Birds called and circled overhead. A few white sailing boats dotted the blue water.

"A disinterested father is a unique kind of hurt," Maresa observed empathetically—so much so it gave him pause for a moment. But then he was distracted by a hint of her perfume on the breeze as she followed him to the villa where their suite awaited. A greeter from the hotel had texted him instructions on the location so they could proceed directly there. "Do you think your half brothers will be glad to see him again? Has it been a long time that they've been apart?"

"Fifteen years. The youngest hasn't seen his father— my father—since the kid was ten." Cameron hadn't thought about that much. He'd been worried about what the other McNeills might ask from them in terms of the family resort business. But there was a chance they'd be too bitter to claim anything.

Or so bitter that they'd want revenge.

Cameron wouldn't let them hurt his grandfather. Or the legacy his granddad had worked his whole life to build.

"Wow, fifteen? That's not much older than I was the last time I saw my dad." Maresa's words caught him by surprise as they reached the villa where a greeter admitted them.

Cameron didn't ask her about it until the hotel representative had shown them around the two-floor suite with a private deck overlooking the lagoon. When the woman left and Maresa was lifting Isla from the carrier, however, Cameron raised the question.

"Where's your father now?" He watched her coo and comfort the baby, rubbing the little girl's back through her pink dress, the bowlegs bare above tiny white ankle socks.

The vacation villa was smaller than the one near the Carib Grand, but more luxuriously appointed, with floor-to-ceiling windows draped in white silk that fluttered in the constant breeze off the water. Exotic Turkish rugs in bright colors covered alternating sections of dark bamboo floors. Paintings of the market at Marigot and historic houses in Fort-de-France, the capital of Martinique, hung around the living area, providing all the color of an otherwise quietly decorated room. Deep couches with white cushions and teak legs and arms were positioned for the best views of the water. There was even a nursery with a crib brought in especially for their visit.

"He lives outside London with his new wife. I spoke to him briefly after Rafe's accident, but his only response was a plea that I tell my mother he's *moved on* and not to bother him again." She stressed the words in a way that suggested she would never forget the tone of voice in which they'd been spoken. Shaking her head, she walked Isla over to the window and stared out at the shimmering blue expanse. "I won't be contacting him anymore."

Cameron sifted through a half dozen responses before he came up with one that didn't involve curses.

"I don't blame you. The man can't be bothered to come to his critically injured son's bedside? He doesn't deserve his kids." Cameron knew without a doubt that he'd suck as a father, but even he would never turn his back like that on a kid.

Maresa's burden in caring for her whole family became clearer, however. Her mother wasn't working because of her battle with MS, her father was out of the picture and her brother needed careful supervision. Maresa was supporting a lot of people on her salary.

And now, an infant, too. That was one helluva load for a person to carry on her own. Admiration for her grew. She wasn't like his dad, who disengaged from responsibilities and the people counting on him.

"What will you do if your half brothers don't want to see your father?" she asked him now, drifting closer to him as she rubbed her cheek against the top of Isla's downy head.

Cameron was seized with the need to wrap his arms around both of them, a protective urge so strong he had to fight to keep his hands off Maresa. He jammed his fists in the pocket of his khakis to stop himself. Still, he walked closer, wanting to breathe in her scent. To feel the way her nearness heated over his skin like a touch.

"I'll convince them that my grandfather is worth ten of my father and make sure they understand the importance of meeting him." He lowered his voice while he stood so close to her, unable to move away.

Fascinated, he watched the effect he had on her. The goose bumps down her arm. The fast thrum of a tiny vein at the base of her neck. A quick dart of her tongue over her lips that all but did him in.

He wanted this woman. So much that telling himself to stay away wasn't going to help. So much that the baby in her arms wasn't going to distract him, let alone dissuade him.

"I should change," Maresa said suddenly, clutching Isla tighter. "Into something for the trip to your brothers' house. That is, if you want me to accompany you there? I'm not sure what you want my role to be here."

His gaze roamed over her, even knowing it was damned unprofessional. But they'd passed that point in this relationship the day before when Maresa had wrapped her arms around him. He'd used up all his restraint then. Time for some plain talk.

"Your role? First, tell me honestly what you think would happen between us this week if I wasn't your boss." He couldn't help the hoarse hunger in his voice, and knew that she heard it. He studied her while she struggled to answer, envious of the way Isla's tiny body curved around the soft swell of Maresa's breast.

"What good does it do to wonder what if?" Frustration vibrated through her, her body tensing. "The facts can't be changed. I'd never quit this job. It's more important to me than ever."

Right. He knew that. She'd made that more than clear. So why couldn't he seem to stay away? Stifling a curse at himself, he stepped back. Swallowed.

"I need to visit my brothers' place. You can relax here with Isla and review the files I started to show you yesterday. Make whatever notes you can to help me weed through what's important." He had to get some fresh air in his lungs if he was going to keep his distance from Maresa until the time was right.

"Okay. Thank you." She nodded, relief and regret both etched in her features.

"When I get back, I'll have dinner ordered in. We can eat on the upstairs deck before we fly back tonight, unless of course, you decide you'd like to stay another day."

Her eyes widened, a flush of heat stealing along the skin bared by the open V of her sundress. He couldn't look away.

"I'm sure that won't be necessary." She clung to her professional reserve.

"Nevertheless, I'll keep the option open." He reached for her, stroking the barest of touches along her arm. "Just in case."

Seven

Just in case.

Hours later, Cameron's parting words still circled around in Maresa's brain. She'd been ridiculously productive in spite of the seductive thoughts chasing through her mind, throwing herself into her work with determined intensity. Still, Cameron's suggestion of spending the night together built a fever in her blood, giving her a frenetic energy to make extensive notes on his files, research leads on Carib Grand personnel, and review her and Rafe's performance in depth. She hadn't found any answers about Rafe's additional activities, but at least she'd done the job Cameron asked of her to the best of her ability.

Now, walking away from the white-spindled crib where she'd just laid Isla for a nap with a nursery monitor by the bedside, Maresa was drawn across the hallway into the master bedroom while she waited for Cameron to return.

What would happen between us if I wasn't your boss?
Why had he asked that? Hadn't she already made
it painfully clear when she'd confided how much she
wanted a kiss in those heated moments in his arms yesterday? She'd relived that exchange a million times already and it had happened just twenty-four hours ago.

Now, lowering herself to a white chaise longue near
open French doors, Maresa settled the nursery monitor
on the hardwood floor at her feet. She would hear Isla
if the baby needed anything. For just a few moments at
least, she would enjoy overlooking the terrace and the
turquoise lagoon below while she waited for Cameron
to return. She would inhale the flower-scented sea air of
her home, savor the caress of that same breeze along her
skin. When was the last time she'd sat quietly and simply enjoyed this kind of beauty, let herself just soak in
sensations? Sure, the beach around the Cap Est hotel in
Martinique was more upscale than the Caribbean she'd
grown up with—public beaches where you brought your
own towels from home. But the islands were gorgeous
everywhere. No one told the beach morning glory where
to grow. It didn't discriminate against the public beaches
any more than the yellow wedelia flowers or the bright
poinciana trees.

It felt as if she hadn't taken a deep breath all year, not
since she'd returned from Paris. There'd been days on
the Left Bank when she'd sat at Café de Flore and simply enjoyed the scenery, indulged in people-watching, but
since coming home to Charlotte Amalie? Not so much.
And now? She had an infant to care for.

If Trina didn't want her baby back—and given the way
she'd abandoned Isla, Maresa vowed to block any effort
to regain custody—Maresa would have eighteen years of
hard work ahead. Her time to stare out to sea and enjoy a

few quiet moments would be greatly limited. Given the responsibilities of her brother, mother and now the baby, she couldn't envision many—if any—men who would want to take on all of that to be with her. This window of time with Cameron McNeill might be the last opportunity she had to savor times like this.

To experience romantic pleasure.

Closing her eyes against the thought, she rested her head on the arm of the chaise, unwilling to let her mind wander down that sensual road. She was just tired, that was all.

She'd nap while Isla napped and when she woke up she'd feel like herself again—ready to be strong in the face of all that McNeill magnetism...

"Maresa?"

She awoke to the sound of her name, a whisper of sound against her ear.

Cameron's voice, so close, made her shiver in the most pleasant way, even as her skin warmed all over. The late afternoon sun slanted through the French doors, burnishing her skin to golden bronze—or so it felt. She refused to open her eyes and end the languid sensation in her limbs. The scent of the sea and Cam's woodsy aftershave was a heady combination, a sexy aphrodisiac that had her tilting her head to one side, exposing her neck in silent invitation.

"Mmm?" She arched her back, wanting to be closer to him, needing to feel his lips against her ear once more.

It'd been so long since she'd known a man's touch. And Cameron McNeill was no ordinary man. She bet he kissed like nobody's business.

"Are you hungry?" he asked, the low timbre of his voice turning an everyday question into a sexual innuendo.

Or was it just her imagination?

"Starving," she admitted, reaching up to touch him. To feel the heat and hard muscle of his chest.

She hooked her fingers along the placket of his button-down, next to the top button, which was already undone. She felt his low hiss of response, his heart pumping faster against the back of her knuckles where she touched him. He lowered his body closer, hovering a hair's breadth away.

Breathing him in, she felt the kick of awareness in every nerve ending, her whole body straining toward his.

"Are you sure?" His husky rasp made her skin flame since he still hadn't touched her.

Her throat was dry and she had to swallow to answer. "So sure. So damn certain—"

His lips captured hers, silencing the rest of her words. His chest grazed her breasts, his body covering hers and setting it aflame. Still she craved more. She'd only known him for days but it felt as though she'd been waiting years for him to touch her. His leg slid between hers, his thigh flexing against where she needed him most. A ragged moan slid free…

"Maresa?" He chanted her name in her ear once more, and she thought she couldn't bear it if she didn't start pulling his clothes off.

And her clothes off. She needed to touch more of him.

"Please," she murmured softly, her eyes still closed. She gripped his heavy shoulders. "Please."

"Maresa?" he said again, more uncertainly this time. "Wake up."

Confused, her brain refused to acknowledge that command. She wanted him naked. She did not want to wake up.

Then again…wasn't she awake?

Her eyes wrenched open.

"Cameron?" His name was on her lips as she slid to a sitting position.

Knocking heads with the man she'd been dreaming about.

"Ow." Blinking into the dim light in the room now that the sun had set, Maresa came fully—painfully—awake, her body still on fire from her dream.

"Sorry to startle you." Cameron reached for her, cradling the spot where his forehead had connected with her temple. "Are you okay?"

No. She wasn't okay. She wanted things to go back to where they'd been in her dream. Simple. Sensual.

"Fine." Her breathing was fast. Shallow. Her heartbeat seemed to thunder louder than the waves on the shore. "Is there a storm out there?" she asked, realizing the wind had picked up since she'd fallen asleep. "Is Isla okay?"

The white silk curtains blew into the room. The end of one teased along her bare foot where she'd slid off her shoes. She spotted the nursery monitor on the floor. Silent. Reassuring.

"I just checked on her. She's fine. But there's some heavy weather on the way. The pilot warned me we might want to consider leaving now or—ideally—extending our stay. This system came out of nowhere."

She appreciated the cooler breeze on her overheated skin, and the light mist of rain blowing in with it. Only now did she realize the strap of her sundress had fallen off one shoulder, the bodice slipping precariously down on one side. Before she could reach for it, however, Cameron slid a finger under the errant strap and lifted it into place.

Her skin hummed with pleasure where he touched her.

"Sorry." He slid his hand away fast. "The bare shoulder was…" He shook his head. "I get distracted around you, Maresa. More than I should when I know you want to keep things professional."

The room was mostly dark, except for a glow from the last light of day combined with a golden halo around a wall sconce near the bathroom. He must have turned that on when he'd entered the master suite and found her sleeping.

Dreaming.

"What about you?" Her voice carried the sultriness of sleep. Or maybe it was the sound of desire from her sexy imaginings. Even now, she could swear she remembered the feel of his strong thigh between hers, his chest pressed to aching breasts. "I can't be the only one who wants to keep some professional objectivity."

She slid her feet to the floor, needing to restore some equilibrium with him. Some distance. They sat on opposite sides of the chaise longue, the gathering storm stirring electricity in the air.

"Honestly?" A flash of lightning illuminated his face in full color for a moment before returning them to black-and-white. "I would rather abdicate my role as boss where you're concerned, Maresa. Let my brother Quinn make any decisions that involve you or Rafe. My professional judgment is already seriously compromised."

She breathed in the salty, charged air. Her hair blew silky caresses along her cheek. The gathering damp sat on her skin and she knew he must feel it, too. She was seized with the urge to lean across the chaise and lick him to find out for sure. If she could choose her spot, she'd pick the place just below his steely jaw.

"I don't understand." She shook her head, not following what he was saying. She was still half in dreamland, her whole body conspiring against logic and reason. Rebelling against all her workplace ethics. "We haven't done anything wrong."

Much. They'd talked about a kiss. But there hadn't been one.

His eyes swept her body with unmistakable want.

"Not yet. But I think you know how much I want to." He didn't touch her. He didn't need to.

Her skin was on fire just thinking about it.

"What would your brother think of me if he knew we…" Images of her body twined together with this incredibly sexy man threatened to steal the last of her defenses. "How could he be impartial?"

Another flash of lightning revealed Cam in all his masculine deliciousness. His shirt was open at the collar, just the way it had been in her dream. Except now, his shirt was damp with raindrops, making the pale cotton cling like a second skin.

Cameron watched her steadily, his intense gaze as stirring as any caress. "You know the way you have faith in your brother's good heart and good intentions? No matter what?"

She nodded. "Without question."

"That's how I feel about Quinn's ability to be fair. He can tick me off sometimes, but he is the most levelheaded, just person I know."

She weighed what he was saying. Thought about what it meant. "And you're suggesting that if we acted on this attraction…you'd step out of the picture. Your brother becomes my boss, not you."

"Exactly." Cameron's assurance came along with a roll of ominous thunder that rumbled right through the villa.

Right through her feet where they touched the floor.

Maresa felt as if she were standing at the edge of a giant cliff, deciding whether or not to jump. Making that leap would be terrifying. But turning away from the tantalizing possibilities—the lure of the moment—was no longer an option. Even before she'd fallen asleep, she'd known that her window for selfish pleasures was closing fast if Isla proved to be Rafe's daughter and Maresa's responsibility.

How could she deny herself this night?

"Yes." She hurled herself into the unknown and hoped for the best. "I know that you're leaving soon, and I'm okay with that. But for tonight, if we could be just a man and a woman…" The simple words sent a shiver of longing through her.

Even in the dim light, she could see his blue eyes flare hotter, like the gas fireplace in the Antilles Suite when you turned up the thermostat.

"You have no idea how much I was hoping you'd say that." His words took on a ragged edge as his hands slid around her waist. He drew her closer.

Crushed her lips to his.

On contact, fireworks started behind her eyelids and Maresa gave herself up to the spark.

Cameron was caught between the need to savor this moment and the hunger to have the woman he craved like no other. He'd never felt a sexual need like this one. Not as a teenager losing it for the first time. Not during any of the relationships he'd thought were remotely meaningful in his past.

Maresa Delphine stirred some primal hunger different than anything he'd ever experienced. And she'd said *yes*.

The chains were off. His arms banded around her,

pressing all of those delectable curves against him. He ran his palms up her sides, from the soft swell of her hips to the indent of her waist. Up her ribs to the firm mounds of beautiful breasts. Her sundress had tortured him all damn day and he was too glad to tug down the wide straps, exposing her bare shoulders and fragrant skin.

Any hesitation about moving too fast vanished when she lunged in to lick a path along his jaw, pressing herself into him. A low growl rumbled in his chest and he hoped she mistook it for the thunder outside instead of his raw, animal need.

"Please," she murmured against his heated flesh, just below one ear. "Please."

The words were a repeat of the sensual longing he'd heard in her voice when he had first walked into the room earlier. He'd hoped like hell she'd been dreaming about him.

"Anything," he promised her, levering back to look into her tawny eyes. "Name it."

Her lips were swollen from his kiss; she ran her tongue along the top one. He felt a phantom echo of that caress in his throbbing erection that damn near made him light-headed.

"I want your clothes off." She held up her hands to show him. "But I think I'm shaking too badly to manage it."

He cradled her palms in his and kissed them before rising to stand.

"Don't be nervous." He raked his shirt over his head; it was faster than undoing the rest of the buttons.

"It's not that. It's just been such a long time for me." She stood as well, following him deeper into the room. Closer to the bed. "Everything is so hypersensitive. I feel so uncoordinated."

The French doors were still open, but no one would be able to look in unless they were on a boat far out in the water. And then, it would be too dark in the room for anyone out there to see inside. He liked the feel of the damp air and the cool breeze blowing harder.

"Then I'd better unfasten your dress for you." He couldn't wait to have her naked. "Turn around."

She did as he asked, her bare feet shifting silently on the Turkish rug. Cameron found the tab and lowered it slowly, parting the fabric to reveal more and more skin. The bodice dipped forward, falling to her hips so that only a skimpy black lace bra covered the top half of her.

He released the zipper long enough to grab two fistfuls of the skirt and draw her backward toward him. Her head tipped back against his shoulder, a beautiful offering of her neck. Her body. Her trust. He wanted to lay her down on the bed right now and lose himself inside her, but she deserved better than that. All the more so since it had been a long time for her.

"Can I ask you a question?" He nipped her ear and kissed his way down her neck to the crook of her shoulder. There, he lingered. Tasting. Licking.

"Anything. As long as you keep taking off some clothes." She arched backward, her rump teasing the hard length of him until he had to grind his teeth to keep from tossing her skirt up and peeling away her panties.

A groan of need rumbled in his chest as the rain picked up intensity outside. He cupped her breasts in both hands, savoring the soft weight while he skimmed aside the lace bra for a better feel.

"What were you dreaming when I first walked in here?" He rolled a taut nipple between his thumb and forefinger, dying to taste her. "The soft sighs you were making were sexy as hell."

Her pupils widened with a sensual hint of her answer before she spoke.

"I was dreaming about this." She spun in his arms, pressed her bare breasts to his chest. Her hips to his. "Exactly this. And how much I wanted to be with you."

Her hands went to work on his belt buckle, her trembling fingers teasing him all the more for their slow, inefficient work. He tipped her head up to kiss her, learning her taste and her needs, finding out what she liked best. He nipped and teased. Licked and sucked. She paid him in kind by stripping off his pants and doing a hip shimmy against his raging erection. Heat blasted through him like a furnace turned all the way up.

Single-minded with new focus, he laid her on the bed and left her there while he sorted through his luggage. He needed a condom. Now.

Right. Freaking. Now.

He ripped open the snap on his leather shaving kit and found what he was looking for. When he turned back to the bed, Maresa was wriggling out of her dress, leaving on nothing but a pair of panties he guessed were black lace. It was tough to tell color in the dim light from the wall sconce near the bathroom. The lightning flashes had slowed as the rain intensified. He stepped out of his boxers and returned to the bed.

And covered her with his body.

Her arms went around him, her lips greeting him with hungry abandon, as though he'd been gone for two days instead of a few seconds. His brain buzzed with the need to have her. Still, he laid the condom to one side of her on the bed, needing to satisfy her first. And thoroughly.

She cupped his jaw, trailing kisses along his cheek. When he reached between them to slip his hand beneath the hem of her panties, her head fell back to the bed, turning to one side. She gave herself over to him and that jacked him up even more. She was impossibly hot. Ready. So ready for him. He'd barely started to tease and tempt her when she convulsed with her release.

The soft whimpers she made were so damn satisfying. He wanted to give that release to her again and again. But she wasn't going to sit still for him any longer. Her long leg wrapped around his, aligning their bodies for what they both craved.

He tried to draw out the pleasure by turning his attention to her breasts, feasting on them all over again. But she felt around the bed for the condom and tore it open with her teeth, gently working it over him until he had to shoo her hand away and take over the task. He was hanging by a thread already, damn it.

She chanted sweet words in his ear, encouraging him to come inside her. To give her everything she wanted. He had no chance of resisting her. He thrust inside her with one stroke, holding himself there for a long moment to steel himself for this new level of pleasure. She wrapped her legs around him and he was lost. His eyes crossed. He probably forgot his own name.

It was just Maresa now. He basked in the feel of her body around his. The scent of her citrusy hair and skin. The damp press of her lips to his chest as she moved her hips, meeting his thrusts with her own.

The rain outside pelted harder, faster, cooling his skin when it caught on the wind blowing into the room. He didn't care. It didn't come close to dousing the fire inside him. Maresa raked her nails up his back, a sweet pain he welcomed to balance the pleasure overwhelming him and...

He lost it. His release pounded through him fast and

hot, paralyzing him for a few seconds. Through it all, Maresa clung to him. Kissed him.

When the inner storm passed, he sagged into her and then down on the bed beside her, listening to the other storm. The one picking up force outside. He lay beside her in the aftermath as their breathing slowed. Their heartbeats steadied.

He should feel some kind of guilt, maybe, for bringing her here. For not being able to leave her alone and give her that professional distance she'd wanted. But he couldn't find it in himself to regret a moment of what had just happened. It felt fated. Inevitable.

And if that sounded like him making excuses, so be it.

"Should I shut those?" he asked, kissing her damp forehead and stroking her soft cheek. "The doors, I mean?"

"Probably. But I'm not sure I can let you move yet." A wicked smile kicked up the corner of her lips.

"What if I promise to come back?" He wanted her again. Already.

That seemed physically impossible. And yet…damn.

"In that case, you can go. I'll check on Isla." She untwined her legs from his and eased toward the edge of the bed.

He wanted to ask her if they were okay. If she was upset about what had happened, or if she regretted it.

Then again, did he really want to know if she was already thinking about ways to back off? Now more than ever, he wanted to help her figure out a plan for her future and for Isla's, too. He could help with that. A pragmatic plan to solve both their problems had been growing in his head all day, but now wasn't the time to talk to her about it.

The morning—and the second-guessing that would come with it—was going to happen soon enough. He didn't have any intention of ruining a moment of this night by thinking about what would happen when the sun came up.

Eight

A loud crack of thunder woke Maresa later that night.

Knifing upright in bed, she saw that the French doors in the master bedroom had been closed. Rain pelted the glass outside while streaks of lightning illuminated the empty spot in the king-size bed beside her. Reaching a hand to touch the indent on the other pillow, she felt the warmth of Cameron McNeill's body. The subtle scent of him lingered on her skin, her body aching pleasantly from sex on the chaise longue before a private catered dinner they'd eaten in bed instead of on the patio. Then, there'd been the heated lovemaking in the shower afterward.

And again in the bed before falling asleep in a tangle just a few hours ago. It was after midnight, she remembered. Close to morning.

Isla.

Her gaze darted to the nursery monitor that she'd placed on the nightstand, but it was missing. Cameron must have it, she thought, and be with the baby. But it bothered her that the little girl hadn't been the first thought in her head when she'd opened her eyes.

Dragging Cam's discarded T-shirt from the side of the bed, she pulled it over her head. The hem fell almost to her knees. She hurried out of the master bedroom across the hall to the second room where the hotel staff had brought in a portable crib. There, in a window seat looking out on the storm, lounged Cameron McNeill, cradling tiny Isla against his bare chest.

The little girl's arms reached up toward his face, her uncoordinated fingers flexing and stretching while her eyes tracked him. He spoke to her softly, his lips moving. No. He was singing, actually.

"Rain, rain, go away," he crooned in a melodic tenor that would curl a woman's toes. "Little Isla wants to play—" He stopped midsong when he spotted Maresa by the door. "Hey there. We tried not to wake you."

Her emotions puddled into a giant, liquid mass of feelings too messy to identify. She knew that her heart was at risk because she'd just given this man her body. Of course, that was part of it. But the incredible night aside, she still would have felt her knees go weak to see this impossibly big, strong man cradling a baby girl in his arms so tenderly.

Not just any baby girl, either. This was Rafe's beautiful daughter, given into Maresa's care. Her heart turned over to hear Cameron singing to her.

"It was the storm that woke me, not you." She dragged in a deep breath, trying to steady herself before venturing closer.

He propped one foot on the window seat bench, his knee bent. The other leg sprawled on the floor while his back rested against the casement.

"I gave her a bottle and burped her. I think I did that part all right." He held up the little girl wrapped in a light cotton blanket so Maresa could see. "Not sure how I did on my swaddle job, though."

Maresa smiled, stepping even nearer to take Isla from him. Her hands brushed his chest and sensual memories swamped her. She'd kissed her way up and down those pecs a few hours ago. She shivered at the memory.

"Isla looks completely content." She admired the job he'd done with the blanket. "Although I'm not sure she'll ever break free of the swaddling." She loosened the wrap just a little.

"I wrapped her like a baby burrito." He rose to his feet, scooping up an empty bottle and setting it on the wet bar. "You may be surprised to know I worked in the back of a taco truck one summer as a teen."

"I would be very surprised." She paced around the room with the baby in her arms, taking comfort from the warm weight. Earlier, Maresa had put Isla to bed in a blue-and-white-striped sleeper. Now, she wore a yellow onesie with cartoon dragons, so Cameron must have changed her. "Did your grandfather make you all take normal jobs to build character?"

"No." Cameron shook his head, his dark hair sticking up on one side, possibly from where she'd dragged her fingers through it earlier. He tugged a blanket off the untouched double bed and pulled it over to the window seat. "Come sit until she falls asleep."

She followed him over to the wide bench seat with thick gray cushions and bright throw pillows. The sides were lined with dark wooden shelves containing a few artfully arranged shells and stacks of books. She sat with her back to one of the shelves so she could look out at the storm. Cameron sat across from her, their knees touching. He pulled the blanket over both of their laps.

"You were drawn to the taco truck for the love of fine cuisine?" she pressed, curious to know more about him. She rocked Isla gently, leaning down to brush a kiss across the top of her downy forehead.

"Best tacos in Venice Beach that summer, I'll have you know." He bent forward to tug Maresa's feet into his lap. He massaged the balls of her feet with his big hands. "I was out there to surf the southern California coast that year and ended up sticking around Venice for a few months. I learned everything I know about rolling burritos from Senor Diaz, the dude who owned the truck."

"A skill that's serving you well as a stand-in caregiver," she teased, allowing herself to enjoy this blessedly uncomplicated banter for now. "You'll have to show me your swaddling technique."

"Will do."

"How did your visit to the McNeill family home go?" she asked, regretting that she hadn't done so earlier. "I was so distracted when you got back." She got tingly just thinking about all the ways he'd distracted her over the past few hours.

"You won't hear any complaints from me about how we spent our time." He slowed his stroking, making each swipe of his hands deliberate. Delectable. "And I didn't really visit anyone today. I just wanted to see the place with my own eyes before we contact my half brothers."

"But you will contact them?" She couldn't help but identify with the "other" McNeills. Her mother had been the forgotten mistress of a wealthy American businessman. She knew how it felt to be overlooked.

"My grandfather is insistent we bring them into the fold. I just want to be sure we can trust them."

She nodded, soothed by the pleasure of the impromptu foot massage. "You're proceeding carefully," she observed. "That's probably wise. I want to do the same with Isla—really think about a good plan for raising her." She wanted to ask him what he thought about buying a house, but she didn't want to detract from their personal conversation with business. "I have a lot to learn about caring for a baby."

"Are you sure you want to go for full custody?" His hands stilled on her ankles, his expression thoughtful while lightning flashed in bright bolts over the lagoon. "There's no grandparent on the mother's side that might fight for Isla?"

"I spoke to both of them briefly while I was trying to track down Trina. Trina's mother is an alcoholic who never acknowledged she has a problem, so she's not an option. And the father told me it was all he could do to raise Trina. He's not ready for a newborn." Maresa hadn't even asked him about Isla, so the man must have known that Trina was looking for a way out of being a parent.

"Rafe doesn't know yet?" he said, with a hint of surprise, and perhaps even censure in his voice. He resumed work on her feet, stroking his long fingers up her ankles and the backs of her calves.

"His counselor said we can tell him once paternity is proven, which should be next week. She said she'd help me break the news, and I think I'll take her up on that offer. I know I was floored when I heard about the baby, so I can't imagine how he might feel." She peered down at Isla, watching the baby's eyelids grow heavy. "I'm not sure that Rafe will participate much in Isla's care, but I'll have my mother's help, for as long as she stays healthy."

"You've got a lot on your plate, Maresa," he observed quietly.

"I'm lucky I still have a brother." She remembered how close they'd been to losing him those first few days. "The doctors performed a miracle saving his life, but it took Rafe a lot of hard work to relearn how to walk. To communicate as well as he does. So whatever obstacles I have to face now, it's nothing compared to what Rafe has already overcome."

She brushed another kiss along Isla's forehead, grateful for the unexpected gift of this baby even if her arrival complicated things.

"Does your mother's house have enough room for all of you?" Cameron pressed. "Have you thought about who will care for Isla during the day while you and Rafe are working? If your mother is having more MS attacks—"

"I'll figure out something." She had to. Fast.

"If it comes to a custody hearing, you might need to show the judge that you can provide for the baby with adequate space and come up with a plan for caregiving."

Maresa swallowed past the sudden lump of fear in her throat. She hadn't thought that far ahead. She'd been granted the temporary custody order easily enough, but she hadn't asked her attorney about the next steps.

A bright flash of lightning cracked through the dark horizon, the thunder sounding almost at the same time.

She slid her feet out of Cameron's lap and stood, pacing over to the crib to draw aside the mosquito netting so she could lay Isla in it.

"I'll have to figure something out," she murmured to herself as much as him. "I can't imagine that a judge would take Isla away when Trina herself wants us to raise her."

"Trina could change her mind," he pointed out. His level voice and pragmatic concern reminded her that his business perspective was never far from the surface. "Or one of her parents could decide to sue for custody."

An idea that rattled Maresa.

She whirled on him, her bare feet sticking on the hardwood.

"Are you trying to frighten me?" Because it was working. She'd had Isla in her care for a little less than forty-eight hours and already she couldn't imagine how devastated she would be to lose her. It was unthinkable.

"No, the last thing I want to do is upset you." He stood from the window seat, the blanket sliding off him. "I'm trying to help you prepare because I can see how much she means to you. How much your whole family means to you."

"They're everything," she told him simply, stepping out of the baby's room with the nursery monitor in hand. When her father left Charlotte Amalie, she had been devastated. But her mother and her brother were always there for her, cheering her on when she yearned to travel, helping her to leave Saint Thomas and take the job in Paris when Jaden dumped her. "I won't let them down."

"And I know you'd fight for them to the end, Maresa, but you might need help this time." Cameron closed the door of the second bedroom partway before following Maresa downstairs into the all-white kitchen.

She was wide-awake now, tense and hungry. She'd been more focused on Cameron than eating during dinner, and she was feeling the toll of an exhausting few days. Arriving in the eat-in kitchen with a fridge full of leftovers from the catered meal that they'd only half eaten, she slid a platter of fruits and cheeses from the middle shelf, then grabbed the bottle of sparkling water.

"What kind of help?" she asked, pouring the water into two glasses he produced from a high cabinet lit from within so that the glow came through the frosted-glass front.

Cameron peeled the plastic covering off the fruit and put the platter down in the breakfast nook.

"I have a proposition I'd like to explain." He found white ceramic plates in another cabinet and held out one of the barstools for her to take a seat. "A way we might be able to help one another."

She tucked her knees under the big T-shirt of his that she'd borrowed.

"I'm doing everything I can to help you figure out why the Carib's performance reviews are declining." She couldn't imagine what other kind of help he would need.

"I realize that." He dropped into the seat beside her and filled his plate with slices of pineapple and mango. He added a few shrimp from another tray. "But I've got a much bigger idea in mind."

She tore a heel of crusty bread from the baguette they hadn't even touched earlier. "I'm listening."

"A few months ago, I proposed to a woman I'd never met."

"Seriously?" She put down the bread, shocked. "Why would anyone do that?"

"It was impulsive of me, I'll admit. I was irritated with my grandfather because he rewrote his will with a dictate that his heirs could only inherit after they'd been married for twelve months."

"Why?" Maresa couldn't imagine why anyone would attach those kinds of terms to a will. Especially a rich corporate magnate like Malcolm McNeill. She knew a bit about him from reading the bio on the McNeill Resorts website.

"We're still scratching our heads about it, believe me. I was mad because he'd told me he'd change the terms over his dead body—which is upsetting to hear from an eighty-year-old man—and then he cackled about it like it was a great joke and I was too much of a kid to understand." Cameron polished off the shrimp and reached for the baguette. "So I worked with a matchmaker and picked a woman off a website—a woman who I thought was a foreigner looking for a green-card marriage. Sounded perfect."

"Um. Only if you're insane." Maresa had a hard time reconciling the man she knew with the story he was sharing. Although, when she thought about it, maybe he had shown her his impulsive side with the way he'd taken on her problems like they were his own—giving her the villa while he stayed in the hotel, paying for the caregiver for Isla while Maresa worked. "That's not the way most people would react to the news that they need a bride."

"Right. My brothers said the same thing." Cameron poured them both more water and flicked on an overhead light now that the storm seemed to be settling down a little. "And anyway, I backed out of the marriage proposal when I realized the woman wasn't looking to get married anyhow. My mistake had unexpected benefits, though, since—surprise—my oldest brother is getting married to the woman I proposed to."

Maresa's fork slid from her grip to jangle on the granite countertop. "You're kidding me. Does he even *want* to marry her, or is this just more McNeill maneuvering for the sake of the will?"

"This is the real deal. Quinn is big-time in love." Cameron grinned and she could see that he was happy for his brother. "And Ian is, too, oddly. It's like my grandfather waved the marriage wand and the two of them fell into line."

As conflicted as Cameron's relationships might be

with his father and grandfather, it was obvious he held his siblings in high regard.

"Which leaves you the odd man out with no bride."

"Right." He shoved aside his plate and swiveled his stool in her direction. "My grandfather had a heart attack last month and we're worried about his health. From a financial standpoint, I don't need any of the McNeill inheritance, but keeping the company in the family means everything to Gramps."

She wondered why he thought so if the older man hadn't made his will more straightforward, but she didn't want to ask. Tension crept through her shoulders.

"So you still hope to honor the terms of the will." Even as she thought it, she ground her teeth together. "You know, I'm surprised you didn't mention you had plans to marry when you wooed me into bed with you. That's not the kind of thing I take lightly."

"Neither do I." He covered her hand with his. "I am not going to march blindly into a marriage with someone I don't know. That was a bad idea." He stroked his thumb over the back of her knuckles. "But I know you."

Her mouth went dry. A buzzing started in her ears.

Surely she wasn't understanding him. But she was too dumbfounded to speak, let alone ask him for clarification.

"Maresa, you need help with Isla and your family. Rafe needs the best neurological care possible, something he could get in New York where they have world-class medical facilities. Likewise, for your mother—she needs good doctors to keep her healthy."

"I don't understand." She shook her head to clear it since she couldn't even begin to frame her thoughts. "What are you saying?"

"I'm saying a legal union between the two of us would be a huge benefit on both sides." He reached below her to turn her seat so that she faced him head-on. His blue eyes locked on hers with utter seriousness. "Marry me, Maresa."

Cameron knew his brothers would accuse him of being impulsive all over again. But this situation had nothing in common with the last time he'd proposed to a woman.

He knew Maresa and genuinely wanted to help her. Hell, he couldn't imagine how she could begin to care for a baby with everything she was already juggling. He could make her life so much easier.

She stared at him now as if he'd gone off the deep end. Her jaw unhinged for a moment. Then, she snapped it shut again.

"Maybe we've both been working too hard," she said smoothly, trotting out her competent, can-do concierge voice. "I think once we've gotten some rest you'll see that a legal bond between us would complicate things immeasurably."

Despite the cool-as-you-please smile she sent his way, her hand trembled as she retrieved her knife and cut a tiny slice of manchego from a brick of cheese. With her sun-tipped hair brushing her cheek as she moved and her feminine curves giving delectable shape to his old T-shirt, Maresa looked like a fantasy brought to life. Her lips were still swollen from his kisses, her gorgeous legs partially tucked beneath her where she sat. Yet seeing her hold Isla and tuck the tiny girl into bed had been...

Touching. He couldn't think of any other way to describe what he'd felt, and it confused the hell out of him since he'd never wanted kids. But Maresa and Isla brought a surprise protectiveness out of him, a kind of caring he wasn't sure he'd possessed. And while he wasn't going to turn into a family man anytime soon, he could certainly imagine himself playing a role to help with Isla for the next year. That was worth something to Maresa, wasn't it? Besides, seeing Maresa's tender side assured him that she wasn't going to marry him just for the sake of a big payout. She had character.

"I appreciate you trying to give me a way out." He smoothed a strand of hair back where it skimmed along her jaw. "But I'm thinking clearly, and I believe this is a good solution to serious problems we're both facing."

"Marriage isn't about solving problems, Cam." She set down the cheese without taking a single bite. "Far from it. Marriage *causes* problems. You saw it in your own family, right?"

She was probably referring to his parents' divorce and how tough that had been for him and his brothers, but he pushed ahead with his own perspective.

"But we're approaching this from a more objective standpoint." It made sense. "You and I like each other, obviously. And we both want to keep our families safe. Why not marry for a year to secure my grandfather's legacy and make sure your brother, mother and niece have the best health benefits money can buy? The best doctors and care? A home with enough room where you're not worried about Rafe being upset by the normal sounds of life with an infant?"

"In New York?" She spread her arms wide, as if that alone proved he was crazy. "My work is here. Rafe's job is here. How could we move to New York for the health care? And even if we wanted to, how would we get back here—and find work again—twelve months from now?"

"By focusing on the wheres and hows, I take it you're at least considering it?" He would have a lot of preparations to make, but he could pull it off—he could relocate all of them to Manhattan next week. He just needed to finish up his investigation into the Carib Grand and then he could return to New York.

With the terms of his grandfather's will fulfilled. It would be a worry off his mind and it would be his pleasure to help her family. It would be even more of a pleasure to have her in his bed every night.

The more he thought about it, the more right it seemed.

"Not even close." She slid off the barstool to stand. "By focusing on the wheres and hows, I'm trying to show you how unrealistic this plan is. I'm more grateful to you than I can say for trying to help me, but I will figure out a way to support my family without imposing on the Mc-Neills for a year."

"What about your brother?" Cam shoved aside his plate. "In New York, Rafe could work in a program where he'd be well supervised by professionals who would respect his personal triggers and know how to challenge him just enough to move his recovery forward."

She folded her arms across her breasts, looking vulnerable in the too-big shirt. "You've been doing your research."

"I read up on his injury to be sure you had him doing work he could handle." Cam wouldn't apologize for looking into Rafe's situation. "You know that's why I came to the Carib in the first place—to make sure everyone was doing their job."

"It hardly seems fair to use my brother's condition to convince me."

"Isn't it less fair to deny him a good program because you wouldn't consider a perfectly legitimate offer? I'm no Jaden Torries. I'm not going to back out on you, Maresa." And she would be safe from the worry of having children with him since he would never have any of his own. That would be a good thing in a temporary marriage, right?

"We'll sign a contract that stipulates what will happen after the twelve months are up—"

"I don't want a contract," she snapped, raising her voice as she cut him off. "I've already got a failed engagement in my past. Do you think I want a failed marriage, too?" Her eyes shone too bright and he realized there were unshed tears there.

She didn't want to hear all the reasons why they would work well together on a temporary basis.

He'd hurt her.

By the time he'd figured that out, however, he was standing in the kitchen by himself. The thunder had stopped, but it seemed the storm in the villa wasn't over.

Nine

Two days later, Maresa sat behind the concierge's desk typing an itinerary for the personal assistant of an aging rock-and-roll star staying at the Carib. The guitar legend was taking his entourage on a vacation to detox after his recent stay in rehab. Maresa's job had been to keep the group occupied and away from drugs and alcohol for two weeks. With her help, they'd be too busy zip-lining, kayaking and Jet Skiing to think about anything else.

The project had been a good diversion for her since she'd returned from her trip to Martinique with Cameron. She still couldn't believe he'd proposed to her for the sake of a mutually beneficial one-year arrangement and not out of any romantic declaration of interest. Great sex aside, a proposal of a marriage of convenience really left her gut in knots.

Leaning back in her desk chair, she blinked into the afternoon sun slanting through the lobby windows and hit the send button on the digital file. She wished she could have stretched out the project a bit longer to help her from thinking about Cam. He'd been kind to her since she'd turned down his proposal, promising her that the marriage offer would remain open until he returned to New York. She shouldn't be surprised that his engagement idea had an expiration date since he wasn't doing it because he'd fallen head over heels for her. It was just business to him. Whereas for her? She had no experience conducting affairs for the sake of expedience. It sounded tawdry and wrong.

Shoving to her feet, she tried not to think about how helpful the arrangement would be for her family. For her, even. He'd dangled incredible enticement in front of her nose by promising the best health care for her brother. Her mom, too. Maresa felt like an ogre for not accepting for those reasons alone. But what was the price to her heart over the long haul? Her self-respect? Maybe it would be different if they hadn't gotten involved romantically. If they'd remained just friends. But he'd waited to spring the idea on her until after she'd kissed him. Peeled off all her clothes with him and made incredible love.

Of course her heart was involved now. How could she risk it again after the way Jaden had shredded her? Things were too murky with Cameron. There were no boundaries with him now that they'd slept together. She could too easily envision herself falling for him and then she would be devastated a year from now when he bought her a first-class ticket back to Saint Thomas. She sagged back in the office chair, the computer screen blurring because of the tears she just barely held back.

Foot traffic in the lobby was picking up as it neared five o'clock. Guests were returning from day trips. New visitors were checking in. A crowd was gathering for happy hour at the bar before the dinner rush. Maresa smiled and nodded, asking a few guests about their day as they passed her. When her phone rang, she saw Cameron's number and her stomach filled with unwanted butterflies. Needing privacy, she stepped behind the concierge stand to take the call. Her heart ached just seeing his number, wishing her brief time with him hadn't imploded so damn fast.

"Hello?" She smoothed a hand over her hair and then caught herself in the middle of the gesture.

"Rafe is on the move with a guest," Cameron spoke quietly. "Meet me on the patio and we'll follow him."

Fear for her brother stabbed through her. What was going on with him? Would this be the end of his job? She might not want to be involved with Cameron personally, but she needed him to support her professionally. She hoped it wouldn't come down to calling in the oldest McNeill brother, Quinn, to decide Rafe's fate, but they'd agreed that Cameron couldn't supervise her after what had happened between them.

"On my way." Her feet were already moving before she disconnected the call. She hurried through the tiki bar where a steel drum band played reggae music for the happy hour crowd. Dodging the waitstaff carrying oversize drinks, Maresa also avoided running into a few soaked kids spilling out onto the pool deck with inflatable rings and toys.

Another time, she would gently intervene to remind the parents they needed to be in the kids' pool. But she wouldn't let Cameron confront Rafe alone. She needed to be there with him.

And then, there he was.

The head of McNeill Resorts waited on the path to the beach for her, his board shorts paired with a T-shirt this time, which was a small favor considering how much the sight of his bare chest could make her forget all her best resolve. He really was spectacularly appealing.

"Where's Rafe?" she asked, gaze skipping past him to the empty path ahead.

"They just turned the corner. Rafe and a young mother who checked in two days ago with her husband for a long weekend."

Maresa wondered how he'd found that out so quickly. She fell into step beside him. "How did you know Rafe was with a guest? I sent him on an errand to the gift shop about twenty minutes ago."

"I hired a PI to keep tabs on things here for a few days."

Her heeled sandal caught on a tree root in the sand. "You're having someone spy on Rafe?"

"I can't assign the task to anyone in the hotel, especially if Aldo Ricci really has anything to do with assigning Rafe the extra duties." Cameron's hand snaked out to hold her back, his attention focused on the beach ahead. "Look."

Maresa peered after her brother and the petite brunette. Her short ponytail swung behind her as she walked. Rafe didn't bring her to the regular beach, but waved her through a clearing to the east. Maresa wanted to charge over there and split them up. Ask Rafe who told him to bring the woman to a deserted beach.

"What's the plan?" she asked, fidgeting with an oversize flower hanging from a tropical bush.

"We see who he's meeting and confront him when he turns back."

"We'll make too much noise tramping through there." She pointed to the overgrown foliage. "I can't believe that

woman is following a total stranger into the unknown."
Why didn't vacationers have more sense?

"He's a hotel employee at one of the most exclusive
resorts in the world," Cameron reminded her, his jaw
tensing as he drew her into the dense growth. "She paid
a lot of money to feel safe here."

Right. Which meant Rafe was so fired. Panic weighted
down her chest. Today, every penny of Rafe's check
would go to extra care for Isla—an in-home sitter to
help Maresa's mom with the baby. What would they do
when they lost that money?

She would have to marry Cameron.

The truth stared her in the face as surely as Rafe
waved at Jaden Torries on the beach right now. Her ex-
fiancé stood by the water's edge with his easel already
set up—a half-baked artist trolling for clients at the Carib
and using Rafe to deliver them off-site so he could paint
them. Rafe was risking his job for...what? He never made
any money from this scheme.

"I'm going to strangle Jaden," she announced, fury
making her ready to launch through the bushes to read
him the riot act.

"No." Cameron's arm slid around her waist, holding
her back. He pressed her tightly to him so he could speak
softly in her ear. "Say nothing. Follow me and we'll ask
Rafe about it when we're farther away so Jaden can't
hear."

She wanted to argue. But Cameron must have guessed
as much because he covered her lips with one finger.

"Shh." The sound was far more erotic than it should
have been since she was angry.

Her body reacted to his nearness without her permission, a fever crawling over her skin until she wanted to
turn in his arms and fall on him. Right here.

Thankfully, he let her go and tugged her back to the hotel's main beach where they could wait for Rafe.

"Someone is using him," she informed Cameron while they waited. "He didn't orchestrate this himself, and he doesn't receive any money. I would know if someone was paying him."

"That woman he just took down to the beach is partners with the investigator I hired," Cameron surprised her by saying. "We'll find out what's going on. But for now, ask him who sent him and see what he says. Do you want me to stay with you or do you want to speak to him alone?"

"Um." She bit her lip, her anger draining away. He was helping Rafe. And her. The PI was a good idea and could prove her brother's innocence. "It might be better if I speak to him privately. And thank you."

Cameron's blue eyes held her gaze. His hand skimmed along her arm, setting off a fresh heat inside her. "We'd make a great team if you'd give us a chance."

Would they? Could she trust him to look out for her and her family if she gave in and helped him to secure his family legacy? Sure, Cameron could help her family in ways she couldn't. He already had. But what would it be like to share a home with him for a year while they fulfilled the terms of the marriage he needed? Still, while she worried about all the ways a legal union would be risky for her, she hadn't really stopped to consider that he was already holding up his end of the promised bargain—helping all the Delphines—while she'd given him nothing in return.

Maybe she already owed him her help for all that he'd done for her. Even if the fallout twelve months from now was going to hurt far more than Jaden's betrayal.

"You're right." She squeezed Cameron's hand briefly,

then let go as she saw her brother step onto the beach. "If you're still serious about that one-year deal, I'll take it."

"Maresa?" Rafe stopped when he spotted her standing underneath a date palm tree.

She was nervous about confronting him, wishing she could talk to him about everything at once. His secret meeting on the beach. His daughter. His future.

But she worried about how he would handle the news of Isla and she wanted his counselor there. The paternity results were in, and the woman had agreed to meet them at the Delphine residence after work today, so at least Maresa would be able to share that with him soon. For now, she just needed to ask who sent him here. Keep it simple. Nonthreatening.

He got confused and agitated so easily. Which was understandable, considering the long-and short-term memory loss that plagued him. She'd be agitated too if she couldn't remember what she was doing.

"Hi, Rafe." Forcing herself to smile, she hurried over to him. Slipped an arm through his. "Gorgeous day, isn't it?"

"Nancy says, 'another day in paradise.' Every day she says that." Rafe grinned at her.

His work uniform—mostly khaki, but the short sleeves of his staff shirt were white—was loose on him, making her worry that Rafe had lost weight without her noticing. She needed to care for him more and worry about his job less. Maybe, assuming Rafe agreed, a move to New York could be a real gift for their family right now. She needed to focus on how much Cameron was trying to help her brother, mother and niece, instead of thinking about how this growing attachment to him was only going to hurt in the end.

Cameron McNeill was a warmhearted, generous man, and he'd been that way before she agreed to help him, so it wasn't as though he was self-serving. She admired the careful way he'd gone about investigating the happenings at the Carib. It showed a decency and respect for his employees that she'd bet most billionaire corporate giants wouldn't feel.

"We're lucky like that." Maresa tipped her head to his shoulder for a moment as they walked together, wanting to feel that connection to him. "What brought you down to the beach?"

Overhead, a heron flew low, casting a shadow across her brother's face before landing nearby.

"A guest wanted her picture painted. Mr. Ricci said so."

Again with the hotel director?

Maresa found that hard to believe. The man had been extremely successful in the industry for years. Why would he undermine his position by promoting solicitation on the Carib's grounds? Why would he allow his guests to think they were receiving some kind of luxury experience through a session with Jaden, whose talents were…negligible.

"Rafe." She paused her step, tugging gently on his arm to stop him, too. She needed to make sure, absolutely sure, he understood what she was asking. "Did Mr. Ricci himself tell you to escort that woman here, or did someone else tell you that Mr. Ricci said so?"

She'd tried to keep the question simple, but as soon as she asked it, she could see the furrow between Rafe's brows. The confusion in his eyes, which were so like Isla's. Ahead on the path, she could hear the music from the tiki bar band, the sound carrying on the breeze as the sun dipped lower in the sky.

"Mr. Ricci said it." A storm brewed in Rafe's blue gaze, turning the shade from sapphire to cold slate. "Why don't you believe me?"

"I do believe you, Rafe."

He shook off her hand where she touched him.

"You don't believe me." He raised his voice. He walked faster up the path, away from her. "Every day you ask me the same things. Two times. Everything. Everyday."

He muttered a litany of disjointed words as he stomped through the brush. She closed her eyes and followed him without speaking, not wanting to upset him more. Maybe she should have asked Cameron to stay with her for this.

She craved Cameron's warm touch. His opinion and outside perspective. He'd become important to her so quickly. Was she crazy to let him draw her even more deeply into his world? All the way to New York?

But as she followed Rafe up the path toward the Carib, watching the way his shoulders tensed with agitation, she knew that his job wouldn't have lasted much longer here anyway. She'd wanted this to be the answer for him—for them—until they caught up on the medical bills and she could get him in a different kind of program to support TBI sufferers. Now, she knew she'd been deceiving herself that she could make it work. In truth, she'd been unfair to her brother, setting him up to fail.

No matter how much she loved Rafe, she needed to face the fact that he would never be the brother she once knew. For his own good, she needed to start protecting him and his daughter, too. Tonight, she'd give her notice to the hotel director.

For her family's sake, she would become Mrs. Cameron McNeill. She just hoped in twelve months' time, she'd be able to resurrect Maresa Delphine from the wreckage.

* * *

Back in the Antilles Suite rented out to his alter-ego, Mr. Holmes, Cameron reread Maresa's text.

Rafe said Mr. Ricci sent him on the errand. Became agitated when I asked a second time but stuck to the same facts.

Turning off the screen on his phone, Cam stroked Poppy's head. The Maltese rested on the desk where he worked. She liked being by his laptop screen when they were indoors, maybe because he tended to pet her more often. He was going to hate returning her to Mrs. Trager when they went back to New York and his stint as an undercover boss was over.

His stint as a temporary groom was up next. He'd been surprised but very, very pleased that Maresa had said yes to his proposal. He needed to make it more official, of course. And more romantic, too, now that he thought about it. Hell, a few months ago, he'd proposed to a woman he'd never met before with flowers and a ring. Maresa, on the other hand, had gotten neither and he intended to change that immediately.

He needed to romance her, not burden her with every nitnoid detail that was going into the marriage contract. She hadn't been interested in thinking about the business details, so he would put them in writing only. It didn't matter that she didn't know about his inability to father children. She was focused on her own family. Her own child. And for his part, Cameron would make sure she didn't regret their arrangement for a moment by making it clear she had twelve incredible months ahead.

He dialed his brother Quinn to give him an update on

the situation at the Carib, wanting to lay some ground-work for his hasty nuptials.

"Cam?" His brother answered the phone with a wary voice. "Before you ask, the answer is no. You don't get to fly the seaplane yourself."

Quinn was messing with him, of course. A brotherly jab about his piloting skills—which were actually ex-cellent. But the fact that they were the first words out of his brother's mouth made Cam wonder about the way the rest of the world perceived him. Reckless. Impulsive.

And his quickie engagement wouldn't do anything to change that.

"I'm totally qualified, and you know it," he returned, straightening Poppy's topknot that she'd scratched side-wise. He'd gotten his sport pilot certification years ago and he kept it updated.

"Technically, yes," Quinn groused, the sound of clas-sical music playing in the background. "But I know the first thing you'll do is test the aerial maneuvering or see how she handles in a barrel roll, so the controls are off-limits."

Funny, that had never occurred to him. But a few years ago, it might have. Yeah. It would have. He'd totaled Ian's titanium racing bike his first time on, seeing how fast it would go. He'd felt bad about that. Ian replaced it, but Cameron knew the original had been custom-built by a friend.

He hated being like his father.

"If I stay out of the cockpit, will you do me a favor?" He thought about bringing Maresa to New York and in-troducing her to his family. Would she look at him the same way when she discovered that he was considered the family screwup, or would she take the first flight back to Saint Thomas?

"Possibly." Quinn lowered his voice as the classical music stopped in the background. "Sofia's just finishing up a rehearsal, though. Want me to call you back?"

"No." The less time Quinn had to protest the move, the better. "I'm bringing my new fiancée home as soon as possible," he announced, knowing he had a long night ahead to make all the necessary arrangements.

"Not again." His brother's quick assumption that Cameron was making another mistake grated on Cam's last nerve.

Straightening, he moved away from the desk to stare out the window at the Caribbean Sea below.

"This time it's for real." He trusted Maresa to follow through with the marriage for the agreed-upon time. "Maresa deserves a warm welcome from the whole family and I want your word that she'll receive it."

"Cam, you've been in Saint Thomas for just a few days—"

"Your word," Cam insisted. "And I'll need Ian's co-operation, too."

For a moment, all he heard was Vivaldi's "Spring" starting up in the background of the call. Then, finally, Quinn huffed out a breath.

"Fine. But the plane better damn well be in one piece."

Cameron relaxed his shoulders, realizing now how tense he'd been waiting for an answer. "Done. See you soon, Brother, and I'll give you a full report on the Martinique McNeills plus an update on the Carib."

Disconnecting the call, Cameron went through a mental list of all he needed to do in order to leave for a few days. He had to have the PI take a close look at Aldo Ricci, no matter how stellar the guy's reputation was in the industry. Cameron needed to make arrangements for a ring, flowers and a wedding. He had to find a nanny, narrow down some options for good programs for Rafe and research the best neurosurgeon to have a consultation with Analise Delphine. He could farm out some of those tasks to his staff in New York. But before anything else, he needed to phone his lawyer to draw up the contracts that would protect his interests and Maresa's, too. He felt a sense of accomplishment that he'd be able to help someone he'd come to care about. This was surprisingly easy for him. As long as they both went into this marriage with realistic expectations, it could all work.

Only when that was done would he allow himself to return to Maresa's place and remind her why marrying him was going to be the best decision of her life. He might have his impulsive and reckless side, but he could damn well take good care of her every need for the upcoming year.

With great pleasure for them both.

Ten

I need to see you tonight.

Standing in her mother's living room, Maresa read the text from Cameron, resisting the urge to hug the phone to her chest like an adolescent.

She stared out the front window onto the street, reminding herself he wanted a business arrangement, not a romantic entanglement. If she was going to commit herself to a marriage in name only, she needed to stop spending so much time thinking about him. How kind he'd been to her. How good he could make her feel. How sweet he was with Isla.

Because Cameron McNeill didn't spend his free hours dreaming about her in those romantic ways. He was too busy investigating business practices at the Carib Grand and fulfilling the legal terms of his grandfather's will. Those things were important to him. Not Maresa.

The scent of her mother's cooking lingered in the air—plantains and jerk chicken that she'd shared with Mr. Leopold earlier. Her mom had warmed up a plate for Rafe when they returned from work, but Maresa's stomach was in too many knots to eat. Huffing out a sigh of frustration, Maresa typed out a text in response to Cameron.

The counselor just arrived. Any time after nine is fine.

She shut off her phone as soon as the message went through to stop herself from looking for a reply. If she wasn't careful, she'd be sending heart emojis and making an idiot of herself with him the way she had with Jaden. At least with this marriage, she knew the groom would really go through with it since he wanted to secure his millions. Billions? She had no clue. She only knew that the McNeills lived on a whole other level from the Delphines.

Here, they were a family of four crowded into her mother's two-bedroom apartment. For now, Isla's portable crib was in Analise's bedroom so they could shut the door if she started to cry. They'd told Rafe the little girl was a friend's daughter and that Maresa was baby-sitting for the night, but he'd barely paid any attention since he was still upset with his sister.

"Mom?" Maresa called as she opened the door for their guest—Tracy Seders, the counselor who would help them tell Rafe about his daughter. "She's here."

Analise Delphine shuffled out of the kitchen, dropping an old-fashioned apron behind a chair on her way out. The house was neat and clean, but their style of house-keeping meant you needed to be careful when opening closets or junk drawers. The mess lurked dangerously below the surface. How would they merge their lifestyle with Cameron's for the next year? Maresa would speak to him in earnest tonight, to make sure he knew what he was getting into by taking on a whole, chaotic family and not just one woman.

"Thank you for coming." Maresa ushered Tracy Seders inside, showing her to a seat in the living area where Maresa had slept since returning from Paris. She'd tucked away the blanket and pillow for the visit.

The three women spent a few minutes talking while Rafe finished his dinner and Isla bounced in a baby seat on the floor, her blue eyes wide and alert. She wore a pastel yellow sleeper with an elephant stitched on the front, one of a half dozen outfits that had arrived from the hotel gift shop that morning, according to Analise. The card read, "Congratulations from McNeill Resorts."

More thoughtfulness from Cameron that made it difficult to be objective about their arrangement.

Now, the counselor turned to Analise. "As I told Maresa on the phone, there's a good chance Rafe doesn't remember his relationship with Trina. He's never once mentioned her to me in our sessions." She smoothed a hand through her windblown auburn hair. The woman favored neat shirtdresses and ponytails most days, and made Maresa think of a kindergarten teacher. Today, the reason for the ponytail was more apparent: her red curls were rioting. "If that's the case, we'll have a difficult time explaining about Isla."

Analise nodded as she frowned, her eyes turned to where Rafe sat alone at the kitchen table, listening to a Yankees game on an old radio and adjusting the antennae.

Maresa repositioned the crochet throw pillow behind her back, fidgeting in her nervousness. "But we don't need to press, right? We can always just end the discussion and reinforce the relationship down the road when he's less resistant."

"Exactly." Tracy Seders tucked her phone in her purse and sat forward on the love seat. "Rafe, would you like to join us for a minute?" she called.

Maresa's stomach knotted tighter. She hadn't told her mother about Cam's proposal yet, but she'd mentioned it to the counselor on the phone in the hopes the woman would help her feel out Rafe about a move to New York. She feared it was too much at once, but the counselor hadn't seemed concerned, calling it a potential diversion from the baby news if Rafe didn't react well to that.

Now her brother ambled toward them. He'd changed out of his work clothes. In his red gym shorts and gray T-shirt, he looked much the same as he had as a teen, only now there were scattered scars in his hair from the surgery that had saved his life. More than the scars though, it was the slow, deliberate movements that gave away his injury. He used to dart and hurry everywhere, a whirling force of nature.

"Ms. Seders. You don't belong here." He grinned as he said it and the counselor didn't take offense.

"You aren't used to me in your living room, are you, Rafe?" She laughed and patted the seat beside her. "I heard your family has exciting news for you."

"What?" He lowered himself beside her, watching her intently.

Maresa held her breath, willing the woman to take the reins. She didn't know how to begin. Especially after she'd hurt his feelings earlier.

"They heard from your old girlfriend, Rafe. Trina?" She waited for any show of recognition.

There was none.

The counselor plowed ahead. "Trina had a baby this

spring, Rafe. Your baby." The woman nodded toward Maresa, gesturing for her to show him Isla.

She bent to lift the little girl from the carrier.

"No." Rafe said, shaking his head. "No. No girlfriend. No baby."

He got to his feet and would have walked away if Tracy hadn't taken his hand.

"Rafe, your sister will watch over Isla for you. But the baby is your daughter. One day, when you feel better—"

"No baby." Rafe looked at Maresa. Was it her imagination, or did his eyes narrow a bit? Was he still angry with her? "No."

He stalked out of the room this time and Analise made a strangled cry. Of disappointment? Maresa couldn't be sure. She'd been so focused on Rafe and trying to read his reaction she hadn't paid attention to her mother. Gently, Maresa returned Isla to the baby carrier, buckling her in to keep her safe.

"Rafe?" the counselor called after him. "I have a friend in New York City I would like you to meet. Another counselor. She lives near where the Yankees play."

Maresa's mother drew a breath as if to interrupt, but Maresa put her hand on her mom's arm to stop her. Analise's eyes went wide while Rafe spun around, his eyes bright.

"The Yankees?" He stepped toward them again, irresistibly drawn. "I could go to New York?" He looked at Maresa, and she realized how much she'd become a parent figure to him in the last months.

"Maresa." Her mother's voice was stern, although she kept her words low enough that Rafe wouldn't hear. "You know that's not possible."

Maresa squeezed her mom's hand, while she kept her

eyes on Rafe. "We could all go if you don't mind seeing a new doctor."

Rafe raised his arm above his head and it took Maresa a moment to realize he was pumping his fist.

"Yankees." He smiled crookedly. "Yankees! Yes."

The counselor shared a smile with Maresa while Rafe went to turn up the radio louder, a happy expression lingering on his face as he sank into a chair at the table.

"Maresa?" Analise asked. "What on earth?"

They both rose to their feet to walk the counselor to the door, and Maresa gave her mother an arm to lean on. Thanking the woman for her help that had gone above and beyond her job description, Maresa waved to her while she walked to her car. Only then did she face her mother, careful to keep Analise balanced on her unsteady feet.

"I'm getting married, Mom." The announcement lacked the squealing joy she'd had when she told her mother about Jaden's proposal. But at least now, with a contract sure to come that would document what she was agreeing to, Maresa knew the marriage would happen as surely as she knew the divorce would, too. "He cares, Mom, and wants to help with Rafe however he can."

Analise bit her lip. "Maresa. Baby." She shook her head. "After everything I went through with your daddy? You ought to know men don't mean half of what they say."

Maresa couldn't have said what surprised her more—that her mother recognized her father had played her false, or that Analise sounded protective on Maresa's behalf.

"I know, Mom." Maresa watched as the counselor sped away from the curb. "But this is different, trust me. I don't have any illusions that he loves me."

"No love?" Her mother grabbed her hand and squeezed—probably as hard as her limited mobility allowed. "There is no other reason to marry, Maresa Delphine, and you know it."

Right. And fairy tales came true.

But Maresa wasn't going to argue that with her mother right now. Instead, she hugged her gently.

"It's going to be okay. And this is going to be good for Rafe. I want us all to move to New York where he can get into a supervised care program that will really help him." She remained on the front step, breathing in the hot air as the moon came out over the Caribbean. Palm trees rustled in the breeze.

"Honey, once you get your heart broke, you can't just unbreak it." Her mother's simple wisdom was a good reminder for her.

She would be like Cameron and look at this objectively. They could be a good team. And just maybe, she could keep her heart intact. But in order to do that, she really shouldn't be sleeping with her charismatic future husband. It was while she was in his arms, kissing him passionately and sharing her body with him, that her emotions got all tangled up.

"I understand," she promised, just as Isla let out a small cry. Her mother insisted on being the one to check on the baby. Before Maresa could follow, a pair of headlights streaked across her as a vehicle turned up her street.

A warm tingle of anticipation tripped over her skin, telling her who it was. What kind of magic let her know when Cameron McNeill was nearby? It was uncanny.

Yet sure enough, on the road below, a dark Jeep slid into the spot that Rafe's counselor had vacated just a short time ago.

Maresa's fiancé had arrived.

* * *

Half an hour later, Cameron had Maresa in the passenger seat of the Jeep. They'd left Isla at her mother's house since the women agreed the baby was out for the night after a final feeding. Or at least until the 3:00 a.m. bottle feeding, which had been her pattern the last few nights.

He'd kept silent in front of Maresa's mom about the fact that he'd been the one to provide that bottle to the baby two nights before. Analise Delphine had been cordial but not warm, unmoved by the bouquets of tropical wildflowers he'd brought for each of them. No doubt Maresa's mother was concerned about the quick engagement, the same way Quinn had been concerned. Both women were worried about Rafe's reaction to his daughter, which had been adamant denial that she belonged to him. Just hearing as much made Cameron's heart ache for the little girl. He knew Maresa would be a good mother figure to her. But how hard must it be for a girl to grow up without a father? Or worse, a father who was a presence but didn't care to acknowledge her?

Of course, one day, she would know that Rafe suffered an injury that changed his personality. But still…he hated that for Isla, who deserved to grow up with every advantage. With a lot of love. Cameron didn't know why he felt so strongly about that. About her. Was it because of the baby's connection to Maresa? Or did he simply have a soft spot for kids that he'd never known about? He'd never questioned his comfort with giving up fatherhood before, but he wondered if he'd always feel as adamant about that.

Now, the breeze whipped through the Jeep since he'd taken the top down. With the speed limit thirty-five everywhere, they were safe enough. Poppy was buckled into her pet carrier in the backseat, her nose pressed to the grates for a better view.

Maresa had shown him how to leave the city and climb the winding road at the center of the island to get to Crown Mountain where he'd rented a place for the night. He hadn't mentioned the destination because they weren't staying there for long, but he didn't want to give her a ring on the doorstep of her mother's home. They might be marrying for mutual benefit, but that didn't mean the union had to be devoid of romance.

She'd had a rough year with her brother's injury and now the surprise baby. And he could tell she'd had a rough evening, the stress of the day apparent in her quietness. The tension in her movements. He wanted to do something nice for her. The first of many things.

"You're very mysterious tonight," she observed as she pointed to another turn he needed to take.

"I don't mean to be." He ignored her directions now that they were close to the cottage he'd rented. He recalled how to get there from here. "But I do have a surprise for you."

She twisted in her seat, her hair whipping across her cheek as she looked backward. "It will be a surprise if we don't get lost since you didn't follow my directions."

"I've got my bearings now." He used the high beams to search for a road marker the owner of the secluded property had mentioned. "There it is." He spotted a bent and rusted road work sign that looked like it had been there for a decade.

Behind the sign lurked a driveway and he turned the Jeep onto the narrow road.

"I'm sure this is private property," Maresa ducked when he slowed for a low tree limb.

"It is." He could see the house now in the distance high up the mountainside. "And I have a key."

"Of course you do." She slouched back in her seat. "I'm sleeping on a couch while you have a seemingly infinite number of places to lay your head at night."

"It helps to own a resort empire." He wouldn't apologize for his family's hard work. "And soon you'll be a part of it. We've got properties all over the globe."

"Including a mountain cottage in Saint Thomas?" She folded her arms, edgy and tense.

"No. I rented this one." He turned a corner and spotted the tropical hideaway that promised amazing views from the terraces. "Come on. I'm anxious to show you your surprise."

"There's more?" She unbuckled her seatbelt as he parked the Jeep in the lighted driveway surrounded by dense landscaping.

Night birds called out a welcome, the scent of fragrant jasmine in the air. The white, Key West-style home was perched on stilts, the dense forest growing up underneath it, although he spotted some kayaks and bikes stored down there. The main floor was lit up from within. Visible through the floor-to-ceiling window, the simple white furnishings and paint contrasted with dark wood floors and ceiling fans.

"Yes and I'm hoping you're more impressed with the next one than you are with the cottage." He stepped down from the Jeep and went around to free Poppy, attaching her leash so she didn't run off after a bird.

"I'm impressed," Maresa acknowledged, briefly brushing against him as she hopped out, unknowingly tantalizing the hell out of him. "I'm just frazzled after the way I upset Rafe down by the beach tonight and then again when we tried to tell him about Isla." She blinked up at Cameron in the moonlight, her shoulders partly bared by the simple navy blue sundress she wore. "It hurts to be the one causing him so much distress after all the months I've tried to take care of him and help his recovery."

The pain in her words was so tangible it all but reached out to sucker punch him. He wanted to kiss her. To offer her the comfort of his arms and his touch, but he didn't want to take anything for granted when the parameters of their relationship had shifted. He settled for brushing a hair from her forehead while Poppy circled their legs.

"They say we often lash out at the people we feel most comfortable with. The people who make us feel safe." His hand found the middle of her back and he palmed it, rubbing gently for a moment. Then he ushered her ahead on the path to the house where he punched in the code he'd been given for the alarm system.

A few minutes later, they'd found enough lights to illuminate the way to the back terrace, which was the main feature he'd brought her here for.

Poppy claimed a chair at the back of the patio and Cam added an extension to the leash to give her lots of freedom to explore. She looked as though she was done for the night, however, settling into the lounger with a soft dog sigh.

"Oh, wow. It's so beautiful here." Maresa paused at the low stone wall that separated them from the brush and trees of the mountainside.

Peering down Crown Mountain, they could see into the harbor and the islands beyond. With a cruise ship docked in the harbor and a hundred other smaller boats in the water nearby, the area looked like a pirate's jewel box, lit up with bright colors.

"Would you like to swim?" He pointed to the pool that overlooked the view, the water lit up to show the natural stone surround and a waterfall feature.

"No, thank you." She wrapped her arms around herself. "It's a beautiful night. I'm happy to just sit and enjoy this." Her tawny eyes flipped up to his. "But I'm curious why you texted me. You said you needed to see me tonight?"

It occurred to him now that part of the reason she'd been tense and edgy on the ride was because she'd been nervous. Or at least, that's how he read her body language now. Wary. Worried.

He wanted to banish every worry from her pretty eyes. And he wanted it with a fierceness that caught him off guard.

"Only because I wanted to make sure we were on the same page about this marriage." He dragged two chairs to the edge of the stone wall so they could put their feet up and look out over the view. "That you felt comfortable about it. That if you had any worries or concerns, I could address them."

Also, he just plain wanted to see her again. Spend time with her when they weren't working. When the whole of the Carib Grand hotel wasn't looking over their shoulders. He didn't want her to feel like he was rushing her into something she wasn't ready for.

"I'm not worried for my sake." She tipped her chin at him as she took her seat and he did the same. "But I'd be lying if I said I wasn't worried about my family. My brother seems excited to go to New York, but my mother thinks it's crazy, of course." She wrapped her arms around herself. "And Isla… I worry that a year is a long time for a baby. How can she help but get attached to you in that time?"

It was a question that had never crossed his mind. But even as he wanted to deny that such a thing would happen, how could he guarantee it? The truth was, he was already growing attached to the little girl and he'd known her less than a week.

"She'll have a nanny," he offered, not sure how else to address the concern. "I've already asked my staff to arrange for candidates for you to interview when we get to New York. And whoever you choose will have the option of returning to Saint Thomas with you if you want to return next year."

"Where else would I go?" She frowned.

"Maybe you'll decide to stay in New York." He couldn't imagine why she'd want to leave. "I've already found a program for Rafe that he's going to love. There's a group of gardeners who work in Central Park under excellent supervision—"

"Don't." She cut him off, shaking her head. Her eyes were over-bright. "We'll never be able to afford to stay there after the year is up and—"

"Maresa." Hadn't he made this clear? The guilt that he might have contributed to her stress by not explaining himself stung. Yes, he'd kept quiet about his inability to father children since they were entering a marriage of convenience, and it wouldn't be a factor anyway. But there were plenty of other things—positive, happy things—he could have shared with her to reassure her about this union. "I'll provide for you afterward. And your whole family. I'm having my attorney work on a fair settlement for you to review, but I assure you that you'll be able to stay in New York if you choose." Maybe the time had come to make things more concrete. He dug in his pocket and found the ring box.

A jingle sounded behind them as Poppy leaped down

from her perch and dragged her leash over to see what was happening. She sat at his feet, expectant. The animal was too smart.

"That's kind of you," Maresa said carefully, not seeing the ring box while she looked down at the harbor. The hem of her navy blue sundress blew loosely around her long legs where she had them propped. "But when you say the marriage will be real, how exactly do you mean that?"

He cracked open the black velvet and leaned closer to show her what was inside.

"I mean this kind of real." He pulled out the two carat pear-shaped diamond surrounded by a halo of smaller diamonds in a platinum band. It was striking without being overdone, just like Maresa. "Will you marry me, Maresa Delphine?"

He heard her breath catch and hoped she liked the surprise, but her eyes remained troubled as she took in the ring.

"I don't understand." Sliding her feet to the stone terrace, she stood. She paced away from him, her blue dress swirling around her calves. "Is it a business arrangement? Or are we playing house and pretending to care about one another as part of some deal?" She spun to face him, her hands fisting on her hips. "Because I don't think I can do both."

Carefully, he tucked the ring back in its box and set it on the seat before he followed her.

"I'm not sure we'll be *playing* at anything," he replied, weighing his words. "My house is real enough. And I care about you or I wouldn't have asked you to do this with me in the first place."

He studied her, looking for a hint of the woman who'd come apart in his arms not once, but three times on that night they'd spent together in Martinique. He'd felt their connection then. She had, too. He'd bet his fortune on it.

"You might think you care about me, but I'm not the efficient and organized concierge that you met when you were pretending to be Mr. Holmes." She folded her arms over her chest. "Maybe I was pretending then, too. I fake that I'm super capable all day to make up for the fact that I keep failing my family every time I turn around. The real me is much messier, Cameron. Much less pre-dictable."

He weighed her rapid-fire words. *O-kay.* She was wor-ried about this. Far more than she'd let on initially. But he was glad to know it now. That's why they were here. To talk about whatever concerned her. To make a plan for tomorrow.

For their future.

"The real you is fascinating as hell." Maybe it was his own impulsive streak responding, but a little straight talk never scared him off. "No need to hide her from me." He reached to touch her, his hands cupping her shoulders, thumbs settling on the delicate collarbone just beneath the straps of her dress.

"Then answer one thing for me, because I can't go into this arrangement without knowing."

"Anything."

"Why me?"

Eleven

It was all too much.

The moonlight ride to this beautiful spot. A fairytale proposal from a man who promised to take care of her struggling family. A man who wasn't scared off by the fact that she'd just inherited a baby.

With her mother's warning still ringing in her ears— that there was no other reason to marry if not for love— Maresa needed some perspective on what was happening between them before she signed a marriage certificate to be Cameron's wife.

"Are you asking me what I find appealing about you?" He lifted a dark eyebrow at her, his gaze simmering as it roamed over her. "I must not have done my job the other night in Martinique."

"Not that." She understood the chemistry. It was hot enough to make her forget all her worries. Hot enough to make her lose herself. "I mean, with all the women in the world who would give their right arm to marry a McNeill, why would you ever choose a bride with a new baby, an ailing mother and a brother who will need supervision for the rest of his adult life? Why go for the woman with the most baggage imaginable?"

As she said the words aloud, they only reinforced how ludicrous the notion seemed. Women like her didn't get the fairytale ending. Women like Maresa just put their heads down and worked harder.

He never stopped touching her, even at her most agitated, his fingers smoothing over her shoulders, brushing aside her hair, rubbing taut muscles she didn't know were so tense. "Let's pretend for a moment that Rafe had never been injured and he was just a regular, twenty-two-year-old brother. How disappointed would you be in him if he chose who to date—who to care about—based on a woman's family life? Based on, as you call it, who had the least baggage?"

Was it Cam's soothing hands that eased some of her tension? Or were his words making a lot of sense? Listening to him made her feel that she'd denigrated her own worth—and damn it, she knew better than that.

"All I'm saying is that you could have made your life a lot simpler by dating someone else." She edged closer to him, drawn by the skillful work of his fingers. He smelled good. And she'd missed him these last two days. "Is that what we're doing, by the way? Dating?"

She wished she didn't need so much assurance. But she'd been jilted before. And she would be making a big leap to follow him to New York, leaving her job behind.

"Married people can date," he assured her, his voice whispering over her ear in a way that made her shiver. "And much more. The two aren't mutually exclusive."

Closing her eyes, she leaned into him, soaking up his

hard male strength. She inhaled the woodsy pine scent of his aftershave, not fighting the chemistry that happened every time he came near her. He tilted her face up to his and she closed her eyes. Waiting.

Wanting.

His thumb traced the outline of her jaw. Brushed her cheek. Trailed delicious shivers in its wake.

When his lips covered hers she almost felt faint. Her knees were liquid and her legs were shaky. She wound her arms around his neck, savoring the brush of five o'clock shadow against her cheek when he kissed her. The gentle abrasion tantalized her, reminding her of the places on her body where she'd found tiny patches of whisker burn after the night they'd spent together.

"You rented this house for the night," she reminded him, her thoughts already retreating to the bedroom indoors.

"I did." He plucked her off her feet, lifting her higher against him so their bodies realigned in new and delicious ways.

"And you haven't even asked me inside." She arched her neck for him to kiss her there, inhaling sharply as he ran his tongue behind her ear.

"I didn't want to be presumptuous." His fingers found the zipper in the back of her dress and tugged the tab down, loosening the soft cotton.

"Gallant." She kissed his jaw. "Chivalrous, even." She kissed his cheek. "But right now, you should start presuming."

He chuckled quietly as he lowered Maresa to her feet again and whistled for Poppy, unhooking the pup's leash where he'd fastened it earlier.

"Let me just grab the chairs." He opened the door for

Maresa and then jogged back to return the furniture to where they'd found it.

Cam was back at her side in no time, hauling her toward the bedroom that he must have scoped out earlier. As if walking on a cloud of hope, she followed him into the large, darkened room where pale blue moonlight streamed through open blinds overlooking the ocean, spotlighting the white duvet of a king-size bed.

It smelled like cypress wood and lemon polish and possibility. Then Cameron's arms were around her again. He slid his hands into her dress, watching with hungry eyes as the fabric slid to the floor and all the possibilities became reality. She hadn't worn much underneath and he made quick work of it now, peeling down the red satin bra and bikini panties that had been her one splurge purchase in Paris. She'd liked the feel of that decadent lace against her skin, but Cameron's hands felt better. Much, much better.

He cupped between her thighs and stroked her with long fingers until she was mindless with want. Need. She felt a deep ache for them to connect in any way possible to help alleviate the nerves in her belly. To ease her reservations about marriage that she desperately didn't want to think about.

Especially not now.

She tugged at his shirt, wanting it gone. But the longer he touched her, the less her limbs cooperated. She couldn't think. She could only feel. Or there was something inherently perfect about only feeling, about abandoning concerns and taking this moment for the two of them, only them, the rest of the world be damned for now.

When the first shudders began, he covered her mouth with a kiss, catching her cries of release. He was so generous. So good to her. He held her while she recovered from the last aftershock. She wanted to return all that generosity with her hands and lips, but he was already lifting her, depositing her where he wanted her on the bed while he stripped off his clothes.

Another time, she would ask him to strip slower so she could savor the ways his muscles worked together on his sculpted body. But right now, she craved the feel of him inside her. Deeply. Sooner rather than later. She waited until he'd found a condom, then sat up on the bed, pulling him down to her.

With unsteady hands, she stroked him, exploring the length and texture of him, wanting to provide the same pleasure he'd given her. He cupped her breasts, molding them in his hands. Teasing the sensitive tips with his tongue. Sensation washed through, threatening to draw her under again. He reached for the condom and passed it to her, letting her roll it into place.

He spanned her thighs with his palms, making room for himself before he thrust into her deeply, fully. She stared up at him and found his gaze on her. He lined up their hands and fit his fingers between each of hers before drawing her arms over her head, holding them there as she took in the moment of them, connected, as one, and a shimmer rippled along her skin.

With the moonlight spilling over their joined bodies, she had to catch her breath against a wave of emotion. Hunger. Want. Tenderness. A whole host of feelings surged and she had to close her eyes against the power of the moment.

He started a rhythm that took her higher. Higher. She lifted her hips, meeting his thrusts, relishing the feel of him as the tension grew taut. Hot.

He still held her hands, her body stretched beneath

his, writhing. He didn't touch her anywhere else. He only leaned close to speak into her ear.

"All mine." The words were a rasp. A breath.

And her total undoing.

Her back arched, every nerve ending tightening for a moment before release came in one wrenching wave after another. She squeezed his hands tight and she felt the answering shock in his body as he went utterly still. His shout mingled with her soft cries while the sensations wrapped around them both.

Replete, Maresa splayed beneath him, waiting to catch her breath. Eventually he rolled to her side but he kissed her shoulder as he went. He brushed her damp hair from her face, smoothing it, pulled the white duvet over her cooling skin and fluffed her pillow. Her body was utterly content. Sated. Pleasurable endorphins frolicked merrily in her blood.

But her heart was already heading back toward wariness. The sex had been powerful. Far more than just chemistry. And she wasn't ready to think about that right now. Not by a long shot.

Yet how long could she delay? Not more than a moment apparently. She didn't have a choice when all too soon she felt Cameron lean over the bed and dig in the pile of clothes. When he came back, he slid something cold along her hand and then onto her left ring finger.

"You should wear this." He left the diamond there and tugged her hand from the covers so they could see the brilliant glint of the stones in the moonlight.

The engagement ring.

She swallowed hard, trying not to think about what it would have been like to have him slide it into place for real, kissing her fingers to seal the moment.

Maresa turned to look at his handsome profile in the

dark, his face so close to hers. He must have felt her stare because he turned toward her, too.

"It's beautiful," she told him honestly, feeling that he deserved some acknowledgement of all his hard work to make this night special for her, even if this marriage might very well break her heart in a million pieces. "Of course I love it. Who wouldn't?"

The words were out of her mouth before she could rethink them. Cameron smiled and kissed her, pleased with her assessment.

But Maresa feared she wasn't just talking about the ring. She was talking about the night and what they'd just shared. Her emotions were too raw and this was all happening way too fast. But somehow, in spite of her better judgment and the mistakes of her past, she was developing deep feelings for him. Very real feelings.

How on earth was she going to hide it from him for the next twelve months? He'd brought her here tonight to discuss their plans for a future. A move to New York. A union that would benefit both of them on paper.

If she had any hope of holding up her end of the agreement to walk away in twelve months, she needed to do a better job of shoring up her defenses.

Starting right now.

Twelve

Two weeks after he first placed a rock on Maresa's finger, Cameron prepared to introduce her to his family. Seated in the third-floor library of his grandfather's house on Manhattan's Upper East Side, Cam sipped the Chivas his brother Ian had just handed him. The three brothers had gathered in the late afternoon to discuss the other McNeill situation before a dinner with their wives, their father and grandfather. He hadn't wanted Maresa to arrive at the house unescorted this evening but she'd been excited to visit Rafe on-site at his new work program during his first full day. It was the first sign of genuine happiness Cameron had seen from her since they'd signed the marriage certificate.

He was trying to give her time to get acclimated to New York before meeting the McNeills, not wanting to make her transition more stressful with the added pressure of a family meeting. He'd even kept the courthouse marriage a secret for the first week—a ceremony conducted by a justice of the peace in Saint Thomas to help keep the McNeill name out of the New York papers. But he could keep things quiet for only so long. Quinn had known a marriage was in the works and finally harassed the truth out of him—that Cam had relocated all the Delphines, including baby Isla, to his place in Brooklyn. Rafe was so excited to see his favorite baseball team play that Cameron had finagled a friend's corporate box for the season, an extravagance Maresa had chided him about, but not for too long after seeing how happy it made Rafe. She didn't know it yet, but Cameron was flying in Bruce Leopold, the Delphines' neighbor in Charlotte Amalie, to attend the team's next home series with Rafe.

Cameron ran a finger over one of the historic Chinese lacquer panels between the windows overlooking the street while he waited for his brothers to finish up a conversation about a hotel Ian had been working on. Cameron felt good about where things stood with all of Maresa's family now. Analise had warmed to him considerably after seeing the in-law suite, thanking him personally for the modifications he'd made so she could get around more easily. It hadn't taken a construction crew long to add handrails to the tub and a teak bench to the shower stall, along with new easier-to-turn doorknobs in all the rooms and an intercom system in case she needed anything.

Isla was sleeping longer stretches at night and Maresa had personally hired a live-in nanny and a weekend caregiver who were settling in well. She seemed pleased with them, and her legal suit for permanent custody of the baby should be settled within the week now that Cameron had gotten his legal team involved to expedite things. Trina wasn't interested in visitation, which made

Maresa sad, but Cameron told her she might change her mind one day. For his part, he enjoyed spending time with a twelve-week-old far more than he ever would have imagined. He liked waving off the nanny at 5:00 a.m. and walking around his house with the baby, showing her the view from the nursery window and discussing his plans for the day. Sometimes, when she stared up at him with her big blue eyes, Cameron would swear she was really listening.

If only his new wife seemed as content. She'd been pulling away from him ever since the night he'd slid the ring onto her finger and he wanted to know why.

"Earth to Cam?" Ian waved his own glass of dark amber Scotch in front of Cameron's nose. "You ready to join us or are you too busy dreaming of the new bride?"

Cam shook his head. "I'm waiting for you to quit talking business so we can figure out our next move with Dad's secret sons."

He wasn't going to talk about Maresa when she wasn't around. He would introduce his brothers to her soon enough and they would be impressed. Hell, they'd be downright envious of him if they hadn't recently scooped up impressive women themselves.

Lowering himself into a leather club chair near one of the built-in bookshelves full of turn-of-the-century encyclopedias that had amused him as a kid, Cameron waited for his brothers to grill him on his fact-finding mission to Martinique.

Quinn took the couch across from Cam and Ian paced. One of them must have hit the button on the entertainment system because an Italian aria played in the background. Quinn must be refining his musical tastes now that he was marrying a ballerina.

"You didn't give us much to go on," Ian noted, pausing

by an antique globe. "You said all three of them—Damon, Gabe and Jager—keep a presence in Martinique?"

Cameron remembered that day of sleuthing well. The only thing that had kept him from feeling resentful as hell about seeing the McNeill doppelgängers had been knowing that Maresa was waiting for him back at the Cap Est Lagoon villa. They'd shared an incredible night together.

"Correct. Jager runs the software empire." They'd all read the report from the PI who'd found the brothers in the first place. "Damon actually founded the company, but he's been noticeably absent over the last six months since his wife disappeared shortly after their wedding." From all accounts, the guy was shredded about the loss, even though he hadn't made the disappearance public. Talking to a few people close to the family about it had made Cameron all the more determined to figure things out with Maresa. "And Gabe, the youngest, runs a small resort property. Ironic coincidence or a deliberate choice to mirror the McNeill business, I can't say."

Frowning, Quinn set down his glass on a heavy stone coaster with a map of Brazil—a gift from their mother. "I thought they were all involved in software? Didn't the PI's report say as much?"

"They are. But they each have outside specialties and interests," Cameron clarified.

Ian took a seat on the arm of the couch at the opposite end from Quinn. He picked up a backgammon piece from a set that remained perpetually out and flipped it in his hand. "Just like us."

Quinn leaned forward. "One obvious way to bring them into the fold is to see if the one who has a resort— Gabe?" He looked to Cam for confirmation before continuing. "We ask him if he's interested in stepping into Aldo Ricci's spot at the Carib now that Cam ousted him.

With good reason, I might add." He lifted his Scotch in a toast.

Ian did the same. "Here, here. Good job figuring that one out, Cam."

Enjoying a rare moment of praise from his brothers, Cam lifted the glass in acknowledgement and took a sip along with them. With the help of another investigator, Cameron had confirmed that Aldo Ricci had been taking kickbacks from low-end artists passing their work off as far more valuable than it was to the guests. With Ricci's worldly demeanor and contacts around the globe, he was someone that guests trusted when he assured them a sitting with a famous artist was difficult to procure.

But for a fee, he could arrange it.

Ricci hadn't just done so with Jaden Torries, but a whole host of artists at the Carib Grand and at properties he worked for before coming to McNeill Resorts. Cameron had released him from his contract and the company lawyers would decide if it was worth a lawsuit. Certainly, there would be public relations damage control. But at least the Carib was free of a man who gladly preyed on employees like Rafe to facilitate meetings—employees who were working on a trial basis and could be terminated easily. Cameron was certain the performance reviews would improve with the manipulative director out of the picture.

Good riddance to Aldo Ricci. The arrogant ass.

"You want to ask Gabe McNeill to take Aldo Ricci's job?" Cameron went on to explain that the youngest McNeill's resort was on a much smaller scale.

"All the more reason to get him accustomed to the way we do business," Quinn insisted. "You know Gramps insists we bring them in—"

A scuffle at the library door alerted them to a newcomer's arrival. Malcolm McNeill pushed his way through the door with his polished mahogany walking stick before Ian could reach him to help.

"I heard my name," the gray-haired, thinning patriarch called without as much bluster as he would have even a few months ago. "Don't think you can conduct family business without me."

Cameron worried to see the toll his grandfather's heart attack had taken on him in the past months. Malcolm had booked a trip to China after initially changing his will, saying he didn't want to discuss the new terms. But having his heart attack while abroad had meant the family couldn't see him for weeks afterward, and they hadn't been able to find out much about treatments or the extent of damage until he was well enough to travel home. It had really scared them.

More than ever, Cam was grateful to Maresa for agreeing to this marriage. Crappy relationship with his father notwithstanding, Cam's family meant everything to him. And even though he'd resented having his grandfather dictate his personal life, it seemed like a small thing compared to the possibility of losing him. For most of Cameron's life, he wouldn't have been able to imagine a world without Malcolm McNeill in it. Now, he sure didn't want to, but he could envision it all too well when he saw how unsteady Gramps was on his feet as Quinn helped him into a favorite recliner.

"We need the women, I think, to really make this a party," Gramps observed once he caught his breath. He peered around the room, piercing blue eyes assessing each the brothers. "Family business needs a woman's touch."

Ian lifted his phone before speaking. "Lydia just texted

me. She and Maresa are waiting for Sofia downstairs before they join us."

Cameron resisted the urge to bolt to his feet, strongly suspecting Maresa would rather meet the other women on her own terms. She was great with people, after all. It was part of what made her so good at her job. Still, it bothered him that he wasn't with her to make the introductions himself.

"Good." Gramps underscored the sentiment by pounding his walking stick on the floor. "In the meantime, Cameron, you can give me the update you already shared with these two." He nodded to Quinn and Ian. "When are the rest of my grandsons coming to New York to meet me?"

Cameron was secretly relieved when Ian stepped in to field the question for him. Maybe, as a recently married man himself, Ian knew that Cam was nervous about tonight. Finishing off the Scotch more quickly than he'd intended, he got to his feet and prowled around the room, looking at antique book spines on the walls without really seeing them.

He was uneasy for a lot of reasons tonight. One reason was that discussion of the other McNeills stirred old anger about his father's faithlessness to the woman he'd married. Cam resented that his father's selfish actions resulted in three other sons and a whole life they'd known nothing about. But, as he now watched his grandfather listen to Ian with obvious interest, Cam had to respect the old man for refusing to limit his idea of family. Gabe, Damon and Jager were all as important to Gramps as Ian, Quinn and Cameron.

It didn't matter that he'd never met them.

For the first time, it occurred to Cam that he had more in common with his grandfather than he'd realized. All his life, Cam had been compared to his reckless, impulsive father. But Cameron would never be the kind of man who cheated on his wife. More importantly, he was the kind of man who could—like his grandfather Malcolm—embrace a wider definition of family.

Because Rafe was Cam's brother now. And Analise's health and safety were as important to him as his own mother's.

As for Isla?

Could he adore that little girl more if he'd fathered her himself? Like Malcolm McNeill, Cameron would never let go of the Delphines. He would use all his resources to protect them. Most of all, he would love them.

The insight hit him with resounding force, as sudden and jarring as the impact of that old kiteboarding crash that had stolen his ability to father children of his own. He didn't need to avoid having a real family for fear of repeating his father's mistakes. He already had a real family and he needed to start treating all of them—especially Maresa—like more than contractual obligations.

Because twelve months weren't ever going to be enough time to spend with her. Twelve years weren't going to cover it, in fact. He needed to make this marriage last and now that he knew as much, he didn't want to wait another second to let her know. Because, yes, he'd always have some of that impulsiveness in his character. Only now he knew he'd never let it hurt the woman—the family—he loved.

"Will you excuse me?" he said suddenly, stalking toward the library door. "I need to see my wife."

"We've been dying to meet you," Sofia Koslov told Maresa in the foyer of the impressive six-story Italianate mansion that Malcolm McNeill called home.

Maresa tried not to be intimidated by the tremendous wealth of her surroundings and the elegance of the beautiful women who had greeted her so warmly. Dark-haired Lydia McNeill, a pale-skinned, delicate nymph of a woman who worked in interior design, was married to Cam's brother Ian. The blonde ballerina Sofia was engaged to Quinn and due to marry within the month.

Both of them appeared completely at home on the French baroque reproduction benches situated underneath paintings Maresa was pretty sure she'd seen in art history books. Cushions of bright blue picked up the color scheme shared by the two huge art pieces. Dark wooden banisters curled around the dual stone staircases leading up to the second floor. A maid had told her the men were on the third floor and they were welcome to take the elevator.

Un-freaking-believable. Maresa had been overwhelmed by Cameron's generosity ever since arriving in New York, but seeing the roots of his family wealth, she began to understand how easy it was for him to re-order the world to his liking. He might have grown his own fortune with his online gaming company, but he'd been raised in a world of privilege unlike anything she'd ever known.

"Thank you." Maresa hoped she was smiling with the same kind of genuine warmth that her sister-in-law and soon-to-be sister-in-law demonstrated. But it was difficult to be so out of her element. Knowing she was going to be a part of this family for only eleven and a half more months hurt, too. "I will confess I've been nervous to meet Cameron's family."

Lydia nodded in obvious empathy. She wore a smartly cut sheath dress in a pink mod floral. "Who wouldn't be nervous? They are the *McNeills*—practically a New York institution." She gestured vaguely to the painting above her head. "This is a Cézanne, for crying out loud. I was a wreck my first time here."

Sofia slanted a glance at Lydia. "With good reason, since we witnessed our first McNeill brawl." She shook her head and tugged an elastic band from her long blond hair, releasing the pretty waves from the ballerina bun. She wore dark leggings with a gray lace top, but her style was definitely understated. No makeup in sight and still incredibly lovely. Sofia turned to Maresa and winked. "Your husband is a man of intense passion, we discovered."

"Cam?" Maresa asked, since she couldn't imagine him getting into a physical fight with anyone, least of all his family. He'd been incredibly good to hers, after all.

Lydia opened her purse and found a roll of breath mints, offering them each one before explaining, "It wasn't really a brawl. But Quinn, Ian and Cameron were devastated to learn that their father had a whole other family he'd kept secret for twenty-plus years. Cam landed a fist on his dad's jaw before they all settled down."

Maresa found it impossible to reconcile her knowledge of Cameron with the image they painted. But then again, he had proposed to Sofia mere months ago in a moment of impulsiveness. Maresa knew he'd gone on to extend the offer of marriage to Maresa because he thought he knew her much better. Because they had a connection. But was she really just another impulsive choice on his part?

Her stomach sank at the thought. No matter how hard she struggled to keep her feelings a secret from him these past two weeks, she feared they'd only gotten deeper. Seeing him walk around Isla's nursery with the little girl in his arms at the crack of dawn the past few mornings chinked away at the defenses she needed around him. How effective were those defenses when just the idea that he'd chosen her in a moment of rashness was enough to rattle her?

Drawing a fortifying breath, she sat up straighter on the bench seat. "He's been incredibly good to me and to my family," she said simply.

From somewhere down the hall she thought she heard the swish of an elevator door opening. Maybe the maid was returning to call them in for dinner?

Sofia flexed her feet and pointed her toes, stretching her legs while she sat. "That doesn't surprise me. We were all glad to hear that he's so taken with your little girl."

Lydia leaned forward to lower her voice. "And for a man who swore he'd never have kids, that's incredible." She reached to squeeze Maresa's hand. "His brothers are relieved you've changed his mind."

Footsteps sounded nearby. But Maresa was too distracted by the revelation to pay much attention. Her world had just shifted. Cameron had never said anything about his stance on children.

"Cam doesn't want kids?" She thought about him singing to Isla in the temporary nursery he'd outfitted for her personally while his construction crew worked to remodel an upstairs suite for her that would be ready the following week.

Had his show of caring been as fake as their marriage?

A male shadow fell over her right as her eyes began to burn. "Maresa."

Cameron stood in the foyer at the foot of the stairs, his face somber. Lydia and Sofia greeted him briefly but he didn't so much as flick a gaze their way before the other women excused themselves.

Maresa stood too quickly, feeling suddenly light-headed at the news that she was being carefully deceived. He'd never wanted children. Did that mean he'd also never wanted a wife? That their marriage was even more of a pure necessity than she'd realized? She felt duped. Betrayed.

And just how many other secrets was her husband keeping from her in order to secure the McNeill legacy?

She cleared her throat. "I don't feel well. If you can make my excuses to your family, I need to be leaving." Picking up her purse, she took a half step toward the massive entryway.

Cameron sidestepped, blocking her path. "We need to talk."

Even at a soft level, their voices echoed off all the marble in the foyer.

"What is there to talk about? Your wish not to have children? Too late. I already heard about it." Hurt tore through her to think she was letting Isla grow attached to him.

"I should have told you sooner—" he began, but she couldn't listen. Couldn't hear him explain how or why he'd decided he didn't enjoy kids.

"Please." She brushed past him. "I spent so many hours interviewing potential nannies and caregivers. I should have devoted more time to interviewing my husband." She couldn't help but remember all the ways he'd stepped into a fatherly role.

All those little betrayals she hadn't seen coming.

"It's not that I don't like children, Maresa." He cupped her shoulders with gentle hands. "I had an accident as a stupid twenty-year-old kid. And as a result—medically speaking—I can't father children."

Thirteen

Cameron was losing her.

He could tell by the way Maresa's face paled at the news. He should have told her about this sooner. He'd disclosed his net worth and offered her a prenup with generous financial terms and special provisions for her family.

Yet it had never crossed his mind to share this part of his past. A part that would have had huge implications for a couple planning a genuine future together. A real marriage. He'd been so focused on making a sound plan for the short-term, he hadn't thought about how much he might crave something more.

Something deeper.

"Please." He shifted his grip on her shoulders when she seemed to waver on her feet. "There's a private sitting room over here. Just have a seat for a minute, and let me get you a glass of water."

She looked at him with such naked hurt in her tawny eyes that it felt like a blow to him, too.

"Isla has to be my highest priority. Now and always." Her words were firm. Stern. But, thankfully, her feet followed him as he led her to the east parlor where they could close a door and speak privately.

"I understand that." He drew her into the deep green room with a marble fireplace and windows looking out onto Seventy-Sixth Street. The blinds were tilted to let in sunlight but blocked any real view. Cameron flicked on the sconces surrounding the fireplace while he guided her to a chair near the fireplace. "I admire that more than I can say."

He wanted to tell her about the realization he'd had upstairs with his grandfather. That he was more like Malcolm McNeill than he'd realized. But that would have to wait and he'd be damn lucky if she even stayed and listened to him for that long. He had the feeling the only reason she'd followed him in here was because she was too shell-shocked to decide what to do next.

He needed to talk fast before that wore off. He made quick work of pouring the contents of a chilled water bottle from a hidden minifridge into a cut-crystal glass he pulled off the tea cart.

"It's not fair to Isla to let her grow attached to you." Maresa closed her eyes as he brought over the cold drink, opening them only when he sat down in the chair next to her. "Even if what you say is true—that you like kids—I should have been thinking about it more before I agreed to this marriage." She accepted the drink and took a sip. "Not that I'm backing out since we signed a binding agreement, but maybe we need to reconsider how much time you spend with her, given that you won't be a part of her life twelve months from now."

The hits just kept coming. And feeling the full brunt of that one made him realize how damned unacceptable he found this temporary arrangement. He needed to help her see that they could have a real chance at something more.

"I hope you will change your mind about that, Maresa, but I understand if you can't." He wanted to touch her. To put his hands on her in any way possible while he made his case to her, but she sat with such brittle posture in the upholstered eighteenth-century chair that he kept his hands to himself. "I never knew how much I would enjoy a baby until I met you and Isla. I never had any experience with kids and told myself it was just as well because my father sucked at fatherhood and everyone has always compared me to him."

She looked down at the glass she balanced on one knee but made no comment. Was she waiting? Listening?

Hell, he sure hoped so.

He plowed ahead. "Liam McNeill is reckless and impulsive, and even my brothers said I was just like him. I've always had a lot of restless energy and I channeled it into the same kind of stuff he did—skydiving and hang gliding. Whitewater rafting and surfing big waves. It was a rush and I loved it. But when a kiteboarding accident nearly killed me I had to rethink what I was doing."

Her gaze flew up to meet his. She had been listening. "How did it happen?"

"Too much arrogance. Not enough sense I wanted to catch big air. I jumped too high and got caught in a crosswind that slammed me into some trees." He'd been lucky he remained conscious afterward or he might have died hanging there. "The harness I was wearing got wrapped around my groin." He pantomimed the constriction. "The pain was excruciating, but I needed to cut myself down to alleviate the pressure threatening to cut off all circulation to my leg."

"Wasn't anyone else there to help?" Her eyes were wide. She set her glass aside, turning toward him as she listened.

"Not even close. That crosswind blew me a good half mile out of the water. My friends had to boat to shore and then drive and search for me. They called 911 and the paramedics found me first." He felt the warmth of her leg close to his. He wanted to touch her but he held back because he had to get this right.

"Thank God. You could have lost a limb." She frowned, shaking her head slowly, empathy in her eyes.

For the moment, anyway, it seemed as though she was too caught up in the tale to think about how much distance she wanted to put between the two of them. Between him and Isla. His chest ached with the need to fix this, because losing his new family was going to hurt worse than if he'd lost that leg. If she chose to stay with him, she needed to make that decision for the right reasons. Because he'd told her everything.

"Right. And that's how I always looked at it." He took a deep breath. "A lifetime of compromised sperm count seemed like I got off easy—at the time. I lost my option of being a father since my own father sucked at it and I was already too much like him. Right down to the daredevil stupidity."

She eased her hand from under his, twisting her fingers together as if restraining herself from touching him again. "Do you do things like that anymore?"

"Hell no." He realized he still clutched the water bottle in his hand. He took a sip from it now, needing to clear his thoughts as much as his mind. "I channeled all that restless energy into building the gaming company.

I designed virtual experiences that were almost as cool as the real thing. But safer. I know life is too precious to waste."

"Then you're not all that much like your father, after all," she surprised him by saying. She set down the cut-crystal glass and stood, walking across the library to the fireplace where she studied a photo on the mantle.

It was an image from one of the summers in Brazil with his brothers and their mother. They all looked tan and happy. He'd had plenty of happy times as a kid and he wanted to make those kinds of memories with Maresa and Isla. Maybe he'd convinced himself he didn't care about having a family because he'd never met Maresa. He'd been holding on to his heart, waiting for the right person.

"That's what I came down from the library to tell you tonight." He crossed to stand beside her, reaching to lay his hand over hers. "It's taken me a lifetime to realize it, but I've got plenty of my grandfather's influence at work in me, too."

"How so?" She turned to face him. Listening. Dialed in.

She was so damned beautiful to him, her warmth and caring apparent in everything she did. In every expression she wore. He wanted to be able to see her face every day, forever. To see how she changed as they grew older. Together.

Cameron prayed he got the words right that would make her understand. He couldn't lose this woman who'd become so important to him in a short span of time. Couldn't afford to lose the little girl that he wanted to raise with as much love as he'd give his own child. In fact, he wanted Isla to be his child.

"Because Gramps would never turn his back on family." He gathered up her hands and held them. "He insists we bring my half brothers to New York and cut them in on the McNeill inheritance, even though he's never met any of them. I was upset about that at first, mostly because I'm still mad at my father for keeping such a hurtful secret from Mom."

"I don't like hurtful secrets." Maresa's eyes still held traces of that pain he'd put there and he needed to fix that.

"I didn't withhold that information about my accident on purpose," he told her honestly. "I didn't give it any thought. And that's still my fault for being too concerned about the physical whys and wherefores of making the move to New York work instead of thinking about the intangibles of sharing…our hearts."

"Our what?" She blinked at him as though she'd misunderstood. Or hadn't heard properly.

"I got too caught up in making this a business arrangement without thinking about how much I would come to care about you and your whole family, Maresa." He tugged her closer, trapped her hands between his and his chest so that her palm rested on his heart. "I'm in love with you. And I don't care about the business arrangement anymore. I want you in my life for good. Forever."

For a long moment, Maresa couldn't hear anything outside of her heart pounding a thunderous answer to Cameron's words. But she wasn't sure she could trust her feelings. She didn't plan to let her guard down long enough for him to shatter her far worse than Jaden could have ever dreamed of doing.

Except, when her heart quieted a tiny bit and she began to hear the traffic sounds out on Seventy-Sixth Street— the shrill whistle of someone hailing a cab and the muted laughter of a crowd passing the windows—Maresa realized that Cameron was still here. Still clutching her hands tight in his. And the last words he'd said to her had been that he wanted her to be a part of his life forever.

That hadn't changed.

And since he'd done everything else imaginable to make her happy these last two weeks, she wondered if maybe she ought to let down her guard long enough to at least check and see if he could be serious about a future together.

Her mind reeled as her heart started that pounding thing all over again.

"Cameron, as tempting as it might be to just believe that—"

"You think I would deceive you about being in love?" He sounded offended. He angled back to get a clear view of her eyes.

"No." She didn't mean to upset him when he'd just said the most beautiful things to her. "But I wonder if you're interpreting the emotions correctly. Maybe you simply enjoy the warmth of a family around you and it doesn't have much to do with me."

"It has everything to do with you." He released her hands to wrap one arm around her waist. He slid the other around her shoulders. "I want every night to be like that last night we spent in Saint Thomas when we made love in the villa at Crown Mountain. Do you remember?"

She remembered all right. That was the night she'd understood she was falling for him and decided she needed to be more careful with her heart. As much as she'd treasured their nights together since then, she'd been holding back a part of herself ever since. Her heart. "I do."

"Even if it was just us, I would want you in my life

forever. But it's a bonus that I get your mom and your brother and your niece." His touch warmed her while his words wound around her heart and squeezed. "Getting to be a part of Isla's life would be an incredible gift for me since I can't have children of my own. But I understand that could be enough reason alone for you to want to walk away. I don't want to deny you the chance to be a biological mother."

She could see the pain in his eyes at the thought. And the love there, too. He wasn't pushing her away, but he loved her enough that he would be willing to give her up so she could have that chance. That level of love— for her—stunned her. And she knew, without question, she didn't need a child of her own to find fulfillment as a mother. She was lucky to have a baby who already shared her family's DNA, something she was reminded of every time she peered down into Isla's sweet face. If they wanted more children, she felt sure they could open their hearts to more through adoption. If Cameron could already love Isla so completely, Maresa knew he could expand his sense of family to other children who needed them.

"I have a lifetime of mothering ahead of me no matter what since Isla isn't going anywhere." She would make sure Rafe's daughter grew up loved and happy, even if Rafe never fully understood his connection to her. He smiled now when he saw Isla, and that counted as beautiful progress. "Isla is going to fill my life and bring me a lot of joy so I'm not thinking about other children down the road. If I was, however, I agree with your grandfather that we can stretch the definition of what makes a family. We could reach out to a child who needs a home."

"We?" His eyes were the darkest shade of blue as

they tracked hers. "Are you considering it then? A real marriage?"

The hope in his voice could never be faked. Any worries she'd had about him deceiving her in order to secure his family legacy melted away. He might act on instinct, but he did so with honest intentions. With integrity. She'd seen the love in his gaze when he'd held Isla. She should have trusted it. He was so different from Jaden, and she'd already let her past rob her of enough happiness. Time to take a chance on this incredible man.

Even when he'd been masquerading as Mr. Holmes, she'd seen the real man beneath the facade. She'd known there was someone worthy and good, someone noble and kind inside.

"Cameron." She pulled in a deep breath to steady herself. "I've been holding back from loving you because I've been terrified of how much it would hurt to let you go a year from now."

He tipped his head back and seemed to see her with new eyes. "That's why you've pulled away. Ever since—"

"That night on Crown Mountain." She nodded, knowing that he'd seen the difference in her since then. The way she'd been holding herself tightly so she didn't fall the rest of the way in love.

She was failing miserably. Magnificently.

"I'm so sorry if I hurt you that night," he began, stroking her face, threading his fingers into her hair tenderly.

"You did nothing wrong." She cupped his beard-stubbled cheeks in both hands. "I just couldn't afford to love a man who didn't love me back. Not again. I went halfway around the world to get over the hurt and humiliation of Jaden, so I couldn't begin to imagine how much a truly incredible guy like you could hurt me."

For her honesty, she was rewarded with a hug that

left her breathless. Cameron's arms wrapped around her tight. Squeezed. He lifted her against him, burying his face in her hair.

"I love you, Maresa Delphine. So damn much the thought of losing you was killing me inside." His heartfelt confession mirrored her own emotions so perfectly she felt her every last defense fall away.

She closed her eyes, swallowed around the lump in her throat. And hugged him back, so tightly, her body tingling with happiness.

"I love you, Cam. And I'm not going anywhere in twelve months." She arched back to see his face, loving the happiness she saw in his eyes. "I'm going to stay right here with you and be as much a part of your family as you already are of mine."

He grinned, setting her on her feet again and sweeping her hair back from her face. "You have to meet them first."

She laughed, her heart bubbling with joy instead of nerves. With this man at her side, the future stretched out beautifully before her. It wouldn't necessarily be perfect or have no bumps along the way, but it was a real-life fairy tale because they would take on life together. "I do."

"And that's not happening today." He kissed her cheek and temple and her closed eyes.

"It isn't?" She wondered how she got so lucky to find a man who loved her the way Cameron did. A man who would do anything to protect his family.

A man who extended that protectiveness to her and everyone important to her.

"No." He cupped her face in his hand and brushed a kiss over her lips, sending a shiver of want through her. "Or at least, it's not happening until the dessert course."

"We can't leave them all waiting and wondering what's happened."

"They'll get hungry. They'll eat." He nipped her bottom lip, driving her a little crazy with the possessive sweep of his tongue over hers. "I have a whole private suite on the fifth floor, you know."

"Of course you do." She wound her arms around him as heat simmered all through her. "Maybe it would be a good time to celebrate this marriage for real."

"The lifetime one," he reminded her, drawing her out of the parlor and toward the elevator. "Not the twelve-month one."

"Or we could wait until we got home tonight," she reminded him. "And we could celebrate it after we tuck Isla in after her last feeding, when we are at home."

"Our home," he reminded her as he stepped inside the elevator cabin. "So you really want to go meet the McNeills?"

"Every last one of them." She didn't feel nervous at all now. She felt like she belonged.

Cameron had given her that, and it was one of many things she would treasure about him.

About their marriage.

"As my wife wishes." He stabbed at the button for the third floor. "But don't be surprised when I announce a public wedding ceremony to the table."

She glanced up at him in surprise. "Even though we're already married?"

"A courthouse wedding isn't nearly enough of a party to kick off the best marriage ever." He lifted their clasped hands and kissed her ring finger right over the diamond set. "We're going to make a great team, Maresa."

He'd told her that once before and she hadn't believed him nearly enough. With his impulsive side tempered by his loving nature, he was going to make this marriage fun every day.

"I know we will." Squeezing his hand, she felt like a newlywed for the first time and knew in her heart that feeling would last a lifetime. "We already are."

* * * * *

If you liked this story of a wealthy McNeill tycoon tamed by the love of the right woman—and baby— pick up these other McNeill Magnates novels from Joanne Rock.
THE MAGNATE'S MAIL-ORDER BRIDE
THE MAGNATE'S MARRIAGE MERGER
And the "other McNeills" stories are coming soon! Meanwhile, don't miss these additional Joanne Rock romances.

HIS SECRETARY'S SURPRISE FIANCÉ
SECRET BABY SCANDAL

Available now from Harlequin Desire!

* * *

And don't miss the next
BILLIONAIRES AND BABIES story
THE BABY FAVOR by Andrea Laurence.
Available July 2017!

* * *

If you're on Twitter, tell us what you think of Harlequin Desire! #harlequindesire

MILLS & BOON®
Hardback – June 2017

ROMANCE

Sold for the Greek's Heir	Lynne Graham
The Prince's Captive Virgin	Maisey Yates
The Secret Sanchez Heir	Cathy Williams
The Prince's Nine-Month Scandal	Caitlin Crews
Her Sinful Secret	Jane Porter
The Drakon Baby Bargain	Tara Pammi
Xenakis's Convenient Bride	Dani Collins
The Greek's Pleasurable Revenge	Andie Brock
Her Pregnancy Bombshell	Liz Fielding
Married for His Secret Heir	Jennifer Faye
Behind the Billionaire's Guarded Heart	Leah Ashton
A Marriage Worth Saving	Therese Beharrie
Healing the Sheikh's Heart	Annie O'Neil
A Life-Saving Reunion	Alison Roberts
The Surgeon's Cinderella	Susan Carlisle
Saved by Doctor Dreamy	Dianne Drake
Pregnant with the Boss's Baby	Sue MacKay
Reunited with His Runaway Doc	Lucy Clark
His Accidental Heir	Joanne Rock
A Texas-Sized Secret	Maureen Child

MILLS & BOON®
Large Print – June 2017

ROMANCE

The Last Di Sione Claims His Prize	Maisey Yates
Bought to Wear the Billionaire's Ring	Cathy Williams
The Desert King's Blackmailed Bride	Lynne Graham
Bride by Royal Decree	Caitlin Crews
The Consequence of His Vengeance	Jennie Lucas
The Sheikh's Secret Son	Maggie Cox
Acquired by Her Greek Boss	Chantelle Shaw
The Sheikh's Convenient Princess	Liz Fielding
The Unforgettable Spanish Tycoon	Christy McKellen
The Billionaire of Coral Bay	Nikki Logan
Her First-Date Honeymoon	Katrina Cudmore

HISTORICAL

The Harlot and the Sheikh	Marguerite Kaye
The Duke's Secret Heir	Sarah Mallory
Miss Bradshaw's Bought Betrothal	Virginia Heath
Sold to the Viking Warrior	Michelle Styles
A Marriage of Rogues	Margaret Moore

MEDICAL

White Christmas for the Single Mum	Susanne Hampton
A Royal Baby for Christmas	Scarlet Wilson
Playboy on Her Christmas List	Carol Marinelli
The Army Doc's Baby Bombshell	Sue MacKay
The Doctor's Sleigh Bell Proposal	Susan Carlisle
Christmas with the Single Dad	Louisa Heaton

MILLS & BOON®
Hardback – July 2017

ROMANCE

MILLS & BOON®
Large Print – July 2017

ROMANCE

Secrets of a Billionaire's Mistress	Sharon Kendrick
Claimed for the De Carrillo Twins	Abby Green
The Innocent's Secret Baby	Carol Marinelli
The Temporary Mrs Marchetti	Melanie Milburne
A Debt Paid in the Marriage Bed	Jennifer Hayward
The Sicilian's Defiant Virgin	Susan Stephens
Pursued by the Desert Prince	Dani Collins
Return of Her Italian Duke	Rebecca Winters
The Millionaire's Royal Rescue	Jennifer Faye
Proposal for the Wedding Planner	Sophie Pembroke
A Bride for the Brooding Boss	Bella Bucannon

HISTORICAL

Surrender to the Marquess	Louise Allen
Heiress on the Run	Laura Martin
Convenient Proposal to the Lady	Julia Justiss
Waltzing with the Earl	Catherine Tinley
At the Warrior's Mercy	Denise Lynn

MEDICAL

Falling for Her Wounded Hero	Marion Lennox
The Surgeon's Baby Surprise	Charlotte Hawkes
Santiago's Convenient Fiancée	Annie O'Neil
Alejandro's Sexy Secret	Amy Ruttan
The Doctor's Diamond Proposal	Annie Claydon
Weekend with the Best Man	Leah Martyn